K19 SECURITY SOLUTIONS
TEAM TWO

—BOOK FIVE—

ONYX'S AWAKENING

USA TODAY BESTSELLING AUTHOR

HEATHER SLADE

MORE FROM AUTHOR HEATHER SLADE

BUTLER RANCH
Kade's Worth
Brodie's Promise
Maddox's Truce
Naughton's Secret
Mercer's Vow
Kade's Return
Butler Ranch Christmas

WICKED WINEMAKERS
FIRST LABEL
Brix's Bid
Ridge's Release
Press' Passion
Zin's Sins
Tryst's Temptation

WICKED WINEMAKERS
SECOND LABEL
Beau's Beloved
Coming Soon:
Cru's Crush
Bones' Bliss
Snapper's Seduction
Kick's Kiss

ROARING FORK RANCH
Coming Soon:
Roaring Fork Wrangler
Roaring Fork Roughstock
Roaring Fork Rockstar
Roaring Fork Rooker
Roaring Fork Bridger

THE ROYAL AGENTS
OF MI6
Make Me Shiver
Drive Me Wilder
Feel My Pinch
Chase My Shadow
Find My Angel

K19 SECURITY
SOLUTIONS TEAM ONE
Razor's Edge
Gunner's Redemption
Mistletoe's Magic
Mantis' Desire
Dutch's Salvation

K19 SECURITY
SOLUTIONS TEAM TWO
Striker's Choice
Monk's Fire
Halo's Oath
Tackle's Honor
Onyx's Awakening

K19 SHADOW OPERATIONS
TEAM ONE
Code Name: Ranger
Code Name: Diesel
Code Name: Wasp
Code Name: Cowboy
Code Name: Mayhem

K19 ALLIED INTELLIGENCE
TEAM ONE
Code Name: Ares
Code Name: Cayman
Code Name: Poseidon
Code Name: Zeppelin
Code Name: Magnet

K19 ALLIED INTELLIGENCE
TEAM TWO
Coming Soon:
Code Name: Puck
Code Name: Michelangelo
Code Name: Typhon
Code Name: Hornet
Code Name: Reaper

PROTECTORS
UNDERCOVER
Undercover Agent
Undercover Emissary
Coming Soon:
Undercover Savior
Undercover Infidel
Undercover Assassin

THE INVINCIBLES
TEAM ONE
Decked
Edged
Grinded
Riled
Smoked

THE INVINCIBLES
TEAM TWO
Bucked
Irished
Sainted
Hammered
Ripped

THE UNSTOPPABLES
TEAM ONE
Furied
Merried

COWBOYS OF
CRESTED BUTTE
A Cowboy Falls
A Cowboy's Dance
A Cowboy's Kiss
A Cowboy Stays
A Cowboy Wins

Table of Contents

1

Onyx

"How was the harvest this year?" I asked my oldest brother, Carlos, more to be polite than because I cared. I'd never had any interest in growing grapes or making wine.

From the time I was a small boy, all I'd wanted to do was become a pilot. I followed a path from the Navy's ROTC program, into college, active duty, Officer Candidate School, and finally into pilot training. Along with flying F/A-18 Hornets, I cross-trained in intelligence and explosive weaponry diffusion.

That training led me to be recruited to work for K19 Security Solutions, a firm founded by four of the CIA's best operatives and agents. Hell, they were the world's best.

It was my job with K19 that took me to South America that fateful day when my life irrevocably changed. I'd come as close to dying as any man ever had when I was shot at point-blank range while flying an aircraft that subsequently crashed.

Sure, everyone said it was a miracle I was alive, but I wasn't. Not fully. I'd lost two parts of myself the minute the shot was fired.

First, my career as a pilot came to an end. The injuries I suffered would never heal well enough for me to fly again.

Second, the organ responsible for pumping blood throughout my body had turned black as coal when Corazón—the woman whose very code name meant heart—fired the gun, intending to kill me.

In the split second when I realized what was about to happen, my eyes met hers and I said what I thought would be my last words. "I love you, Corazón."

She'd pulled the trigger anyway.

That was one year ago today, and in that time, I'd spent a month in a coma and four months learning to walk again. Learning to love again was something I'd never be able to do. I didn't want to.

"Montano? Did you hear me?" Carlos asked.

"What did you say?"

He laughed and reached over to pat my shoulder. "It doesn't matter. I know you never cared much about the vineyards."

"Sorry, man. I got lost in thought for a minute."

He nodded as though he understood. "Can you believe how big all these kids have gotten?"

"I can't." I'd spent so little time around my family over the past few years, I couldn't remember the last time we'd all spent Thanksgiving together.

With five brothers and three sisters, all of whom, besides me, were married with kids, my parents' place in Paso Robles, while large enough to raise us all, was a madhouse this year. Even though it was normally chilly this close to the Pacific Ocean, today was warm enough that we could be outdoors.

My sister Erlinda walked over to the side yard where my brother and I sat chatting. "Would you like more wine?"

I looked at my half-full glass. "I'm good."

As she walked away, Carlos cleared his throat and held up his drink. "Ahem."

"*You* didn't almost die. You can get your own," Erlinda said over her shoulder.

I watched my siblings' kids as they ran around the large grassy area behind the house. When we were their age, there didn't seem to be much time for playing. Even on holidays, there was work to do in the vineyards that sat on our parents' property but were leased by my cousins, the Avilas, for their Los Caballeros Winery.

"Montano?" Mama called my name from the front yard.

"Someone actually expects you to get off your ass?" Carlos muttered, but I knew he was joking. He'd been there, along with my closest friend, Monk, through weeks of agonizing rehab when I was forced to work my body harder than I ever had.

"There's someone here to see you," she added.

I rounded the corner of the yard to the front of the house and gripped the porch's railing when I saw the ghost that stood before me. *"Corazón?"*

"Corazón? Um, no, my name is Blanca Descanso."

Simple words. A statement of fact. Yet, I could tell by the look on the woman's face that she saw the pain speaking them caused me.

"I'm sorry…It hasn't been easy to find you."

I took the deepest breath I could, trying to refill my lungs with enough air to speak again. "Who are you?"

"Sofia Descanso was my sister."

"Montano, introduce your friend to everyone," said my mother, who I was sure had been hovering close enough to hear the few words the woman and I had spoken to one another. When she put her arm through mine, I was grateful for the strength that flowed from her into me.

"This is Blanca."

"I am Esmeralda. Welcome to our home, Blanca."

"Thank you, Esmeralda," said the woman whose voice sounded so much like her sister's that every word she spoke felt like a knife in my heart.

"Call me Mama, everyone does." My mother released my arm and motioned to the woman to follow her. "Come, we're just about to sit down for dinner."

"Oh, I couldn't. I don't want to intrude."

"You already have," my mother responded but with a wink to soften what Blanca could've taken as rude.

She looked at me, perhaps hoping I'd intervene with my mother on her behalf, but I said nothing.

I walked beside them and studied her without bothering to hide I was. She looked so much like Corazón, I wondered if they were twins. *Not Corazón—Sofia.* While I'd referred to her as my heart, the woman hadn't ever truly been.

Should I tell Blanca that in the weeks and months her sister and I had spent together, she never once mentioned a sibling? She said it hadn't been easy to find me. How long had she been looking? More perplexing, who told her how to do so?

She looked at the table where my siblings were setting platters of food. "I forgot," she mumbled. Her brow furrowed and her eyes met mine.

"What did you forget?"

She raised one hand to her cheek. "That it's Thanksgiving. I haven't celebrated the holiday in so long."

"Your family doesn't celebrate Thanksgiving?" asked my eavesdropping mother.

"Um…There isn't anyone left."

I took another step closer when her cheeks turned red and it appeared she might cry. "Come with me."

I took her hand and led her away from the prying eyes of my relatives. I knew her mother had passed away when Sofia was a teenager, but I had no idea her father had also died.

"I'm sorry to hear about your dad," I said without releasing my grasp. "When did it happen?"

"A month ago." She looked down at our hands, and I let go. "It's why I came back."

"Came back?"

"I've been living overseas."

The expression was outdated and only used by a certain segment of the population. "Military?"

"My father was."

I nodded, remembering then that he had been in the Army.

"I left home when I was eighteen." She took a deep breath and let it out slowly. "My family and I were…estranged."

"Montano, come and eat," my sister Erlinda hollered, waving at me.

"They won't start without us."

"I really should go."

"Where you gonna go?" I asked.

"What do you mean?"

"I know you don't have another Thanksgiving dinner to attend since you forgot today was a holiday, sis."

"Sis?"

"Just a thing I do. Come on." I took the same hand I held before. When we got to the long tables set up on the back lawn, there were only two open seats. I motioned for Blanca to precede me and helped with her chair.

"Thank you," she said, her eyes meeting mine again.

"Montano, do you want to say grace?" asked my mother.

I laughed at the look of annoyance on my oldest brother's face, the man seated at the head of the table. "Go ahead, Carlos."

He cleared his throat and motioned for us all to hold hands. "Lord, bless this gathering of our family, a circle of strength and love.

"We are fathers, mothers, sisters, brothers, aunts, uncles, cousins, and friends. With every marriage and every birth, the circle grows. Every joy shared adds more love. Every crisis faced together makes the circle stronger.

"Look down on us, Lord, and surround us all with your divine guidance and love. We thank you for the many blessings and great abundance in our lives. As we gather to celebrate this Thanksgiving, we are particularly thankful for the presence of our brother Montano and his friend Blanca. Amen."

"Thank you," I mouthed to him.

"It all smells so good," she said as the dishes came around. "Not hungry?" she asked, looking at my near-empty plate.

I leaned back and patted my stomach. "Too many jalapeño poppers."

"That's why they were all gone," said my sister Jada, who sat on the other side of me. When she elbowed me, I let out a cry that made her turn ghostly white.

"Montano, I'm—"

I nudged her in return. "I'm just joshing with you, sis."

When she tried to swat me, I leaned back too far and bumped into Blanca. "She made me do it," I said, turning to apologize. Before I could speak, though, her beauty took my breath away.

Sure, she looked like Sofia, but there was more. Only now did I realize the shallowness of the eyes I'd peered into so often. In contrast, Blanca's possessed a warmth that made me want to swim in their deep, dark richness.

"What?" she asked, reaching up to tuck a piece of hair behind her ear.

I leaned closer. "Your eyes…are beautiful."

Her gaze remained on mine as she passed the bowl of chorizo stuffing. "I'm sorry. I know I remind you of her." She shook her head. "I shouldn't have come."

"Why *did* you?" I asked, still close enough that I could speak without my boisterous family overhearing.

Blanca rested her fork on her plate. "I just…" She looked around and gave a small shake of her head.

I took the bowl with my left hand and patted hers with my right. "We'll talk later."

My mother and sisters had really outdone themselves. Besides turkey and stuffing, they'd prepared pork tamales, sweet potato black-bean enchiladas, roasted zucchini, and mashed potatoes. For dessert, there were pumpkin empañadas, pumpkin pie tamales, and my mother's signature Mexican hot chocolate cookies.

When Blanca said my family should open a restaurant, I was plagued by conversations I'd had with her sister on the subject. More than continuing her career as a pilot, Sofia had wanted to be a chef.

Blanca leaned in my direction, perhaps picking up on my darkened mood. "I hope I didn't say the wrong thing. It's just that the food is all so delicious."

I shook my head as much to get her sister out of it as to reassure Blanca. "It isn't that."

"Okay. Well, I'm sorry."

"Don't be."

She scooted her chair away from the table. "I should be going."

"Going? You aren't staying to help clean up?"

She gasped. "You must think I'm so rude. *Of course* I'll help."

I tried to keep a straight face, but her look of horror made me laugh out loud. "I'm just joshing you, sis."

"Sis," she said again, but not as a question this time.

"He does that to everyone," said Jada. "Be glad he didn't call you bro or dude. That's what he usually calls me."

"Where are you staying?" I asked.

"Not far from here. In a guesthouse at Los Caballeros Winery."

"My cousins own Los Cab."

"Really?"

"Really, sis—sorry."

She shrugged one shoulder. "I guess there was a chance I might've been your sister-in-law."

"No," I said both too quickly and emphatically.

Her cheeks flushed. "I'm sorry," she repeated. "I keep saying the wrong thing."

"It isn't you," I said, turning my head to look in the opposite direction. "Some things sit too close to the surface."

"That, I understand."

"Feel like taking a walk?"

"Um…sure. As long as your mother won't think I'm ungrateful."

"I was just joking earlier. No way my mama would let a guest help clean up. Come on." I pushed my chair back like she had.

"Earlier, you asked why I came," she said once we were a good distance from my family.

"I did."

"Looking for answers, I suppose. Sofia wasn't just my sister. I'm sure you guessed she was my twin. I know it sounds crazy, but even though we hadn't spoken in years, I knew when she died."

I nodded, doing my best to keep the nightmarish events of that day from replaying in my head.

"I know it must be hard for you too. Did you…I mean…were you…"

I could prompt her, help her formulate the question that might be hard for her to ask, but coming up with an answer would be even more difficult for me.

"My father said he thought you and Sofia might marry someday."

I looked out over the rolling hills covered with the grapes my family tended. "I can't say whether we would have or not." In my line of work, "can't say" meant something different than Blanca would likely assume.

"That was my father's line when there was something he didn't want to—or couldn't—talk about." She smirked and I chuckled.

"You got me there." When we reached a crest in the vineyards, I pointed to a bench and we took a seat. My legs were stiff from inactivity, made more evident by the short walk uphill.

"It's so beautiful here," she murmured, looking out at the view that stretched all the way to the ocean.

"Growing up here, I didn't appreciate it."

"No? Do you now?"

"I guess I do." I glanced in her direction. "How long will you be in town?" I asked rather than prompting her again to tell me why she was here. While she hadn't elaborated, saying she was looking for answers was enough. The information she sought about her sister's death would never be forthcoming, even to her family; it was classified.

"I haven't made up my mind."

There were countless things I would say under a different circumstance—one where the beautiful woman seated beside me wasn't the identical twin of my would-be murderer. I might suggest reasons why she should stick around, some of which would include offering to keep her bed warm when the chill of the ocean breezes sent the nighttime temperatures plummeting. That I didn't, only served as proof of how much the woman's sister had shredded me. I was Latin, for God's sake. I'd been successfully seducing the opposite sex since I reached puberty.

When I rested my arm on the back of the bench, I felt pulled to touch Blanca's bare shoulder, itching to trail my fingertips up the side of her neck. Instead, I gripped the old wood hard enough that I felt the sting of splinters in my palm. *Pain.* It was a constant reminder of how much my life had changed. Not just my life—me.

2

Blanca

I shouldn't have come. More, I should've left. Not agreed to have dinner with his family. *God— Thanksgiving dinner.* Even now, recognizing all of my should-haves, I couldn't bring myself to get up from this bench, thank the man and then his family for their hospitality, and leave.

When Montano asked how long I'd be in town, I told him I hadn't made up my mind. The truth was, I was scheduled to leave for New York tomorrow night.

The thought of doing so made my heart hurt. But why? Was it because he had a connection to my twin? Did the longing I felt so strongly come from the loss of the person who had been part of me in a way that no other human ever could be?

Was it Sofia's arms I yearned to feel wrapping me in a hug or her voice I ached to hear tell me the reports of her death had been a horrible mistake? Or was it that I so desperately needed comfort that I almost couldn't help myself from resting my head on Montano's shoulder?

I took a deep breath and leaned against the bench. When I felt Montano's arm there, I bolted upright.

He put his hand on my shoulder. "Relax," he whispered. "I don't bite."

When I allowed myself to do as he suggested, it was his hand still touching me that not only loosened my muscles but filled me with a sense of peace.

"I'm here because I hoped you'd tell me what you know about my sister. Both about the plane crash and about her life these last few years."

When he moved his hand from my shoulder, I felt an inexplicable chill, powerful enough that I shuddered. While he didn't put it back, I could feel his fingers twining the ends of my long hair.

I instinctively prepared myself when he took a deep breath. Why did I assume he was going to tell me something bad?

Before he could respond, my cell phone rang. "Sorry," I muttered, answering even though I didn't recognize the number.

"Ms. Descanso, this is Brix…err…Gabe Avila."

"Hello," I repeated.

"I'm calling to let you know someone stopped by the ranch, looking for you, a couple of hours ago. He didn't leave a name."

Someone was looking for me? Who would be looking for me?

"Are you still there?"

"Yes, sorry, um, could you describe him?"

"I didn't see him. That's why I didn't contact you sooner. My brother Rascon mentioned it a little while ago. I can ask what he remembers about the guy."

"I'd appreciate it."

"Sure, uh, my mother is asking what time we should expect you."

"I should be there within the hour."

"I'll still be here, so I'll let you know what my brother says when you arrive."

I thanked him and ended the call. When I looked at Montano, he was studying me.

"That was someone from Los Caballeros. He said his name was Gabe or Brix or something like that."

"My cousin. His name is Gabe, but everyone calls him Brix."

"Right. That's what he said."

"Brix is how the sugar content of something—wine, for example—is measured."

I nodded, not really paying attention to what he was saying. My mind raced with who would've been looking for me. There was literally no one I could come up with. That whomever it was knew I was staying the night in the winery's guesthouse further perplexed me.

"Everything okay, sis?"

I didn't comment on his use of sis; apparently, it was something he did without thinking.

"Yes," I said, looking up at him. "I really should be going." Something told me he wouldn't mind my leaving without giving him the chance to talk about my sister. In fact, I sensed he'd be relieved not to have to do so.

"Come on. Fess up. Something about that conversation troubled you."

"I'm not sure troubled is the right word for it."

"What would be?"

I shrugged. Maybe his word choice was dead-on. "Your cousin said someone stopped by, looking for me."

"Did he say who it was?"

"The man didn't leave a name."

"Do you know people in the area?"

"Not a soul."

"Ouch."

My eyes met his. "What?"

"You know me. My family too."

I questioned his word choice a second time. I didn't *know* him or his family and doubted I ever would. "I'll just go and offer my appreciation and then be on my way."

"We didn't have time to talk."

"I got the impression you didn't want to."

While I waited for his response, I studied him like I'd found him doing to me several times since I arrived. It was easy to see why my sister fell for him.

The man possessed classic good looks with a straight Greek nose, powerful jawline, and high cheekbones any woman would envy. His hazel eyes had changed from brown to green to blue in the time since I first looked into them.

He was tall, probably close to six and a half feet, with a physique that could only be achieved with daily workouts. He wasn't overly muscular, though. Just the right amount. Everything about him appeared to be practically perfect as my eyes traveled from his head, down his body, and back up again.

"I'd ask if you like what you see," he said with a mercurial grin. "But that much is obvious."

My cheeks heated in embarrassment. "Sorry. I didn't mean to make you feel uncomfortable."

"Not at all. In fact, I do too."

The sudden realization that I was flirting with my dead sister's boyfriend, and he was reciprocating, turned my stomach. What was wrong with me?

"I really must be going."

"I'll walk you back."

"That isn't necessary."

"Of course it is."

When our hands brushed, I folded my arms so it wouldn't happen again. The smile left his face, and he looked away. Perhaps my pulling away brought him to the same realization I'd come to.

"There's something you could do for me," said Montano's mother when I thanked her.

"Um, sure. Of course."

"Please take this to my sister," she said, handing me a plate covered with aluminum foil.

"Your sister?"

"You're staying at Los Caballeros, yes?"

"I am."

"Lucia Avila is my older sister." Montano raised a brow, and his mother laughed. "Actually, I'm older, but only by two minutes."

"You're twins?" I gasped. "I'm a twin too. Was. My sister died."

Esmeralda tucked her arm in mine and walked with me to my rental car. "I understand your loss in ways very few can. If you ever feel like talking, you know where I am."

"Mama," said Montano with a furrowed brow.

His mother leaned closer to me. "As I said, few understand."

"How long will you be in town?" he asked like he had earlier.

Then, I told him I wasn't sure. Now, I was. "I'm leaving tomorrow afternoon."

"So soon? Where to?"

"Our family owns a camp in the Adirondacks. I guess it doesn't belong to my family anymore; it's mine now. Anyway, we used to spend time there every summer. Some of my best childhood memories are of the lake."

"With Sofia?"

"Yes," I whispered, looking away when I felt my eyes fill with tears.

Montano took my hand in his. "I hope you find happy memories while you're there."

"Thank you. I do too."

"Which lake?"

"Are you familiar with the area?"

"Somewhat. A guy I work with has a place on Canada Lake. It's been in his family for several generations."

"You're kidding."

"About which part?"

"Canada Lake."

"Nope, not kidding, sis."

"Our camp—cottage—is on the same lake."

"Ranger loves the place. I've been once, but every year he invites me back."

"Ranger?"

"Owen Messick. A, uh, buddy of mine."

"You're kidding," I repeated. "The Messicks?"

"Yeah. You know 'em?"

"Know them? Their camp is next door to ours. If it's the same Messicks. Does Owen have a brother named Jimmy?"

"Sure does. By the look on your face, I'd say Jimmy was more than an acquaintance."

He sure was, not that I'd get into the particulars of my first love with Montano. Before I could respond, though, the light in his eyes darkened. "You or Sofia?"

"Me," I answered, probably too quickly. If I'd expected that news to make him feel better, I would have been wrong. The scowl on his face remained. "He wasn't my sister's type."

"But he was yours?"

I smiled. "Definitely." If I closed my eyes, which I wouldn't do now, I could still see how he looked back when we were both fifteen. Not just that. I could still recall the taste of his lips when he gave me my first kiss. A girl doesn't forget her first kiss. Not ever.

"He's married," Montano blurted and I laughed.

"Not why I'm going to the lake, but thanks for the heads-up."

He squeezed my hand but didn't let go. "If you change your mind about telling me why you came, you know where to find me. Actually, I won't be here. By the way, how did you find me?"

I wriggled my hand free of his grasp. "Um, I'm not supposed to tell you." I didn't think it was possible, but his face darkened more.

"How?" he snapped.

"I found a piece of paper with a name and number on it. When I called, a woman who said she was the man's wife told me she thought you'd be here. As soon as she did, I think she regretted it."

His eyes scrunched. "Who?"

I promised her I wouldn't tell, but based on Montano's reaction, I knew I had to. "She said her name was Malin."

He nodded, and as he did, the tension I saw on his face slowly disappeared. "She knows better," he mumbled.

"I'm sorry."

"Don't be."

"Okay. Well, have a nice life." It sounded lame, but I was at a loss for what else to say.

Montano's smile nearly stopped my heart. "You too," he said, closing the door after I got into the car.

3

Onyx

A nice life. Not a chance of that, I thought as I watched Blanca's car pull out of the gates of our ranch. Her sister had made sure I wouldn't. But that wasn't Blanca's fault. From what little she'd said, it was evident she and Sofia weren't close for the last few years. Close? Hell, it sounded like they didn't even speak.

And Malin? What the fuck? She'd been with the CIA longer than I had. She knew better than to divulge someone's location.

My cell rang, and I answered when I saw it was Doc Butler calling.

"Happy Thanksgiving," I said when I accepted the call.

"Same to you. Gotta tell you, being able to hear your voice this year is something I'm damned thankful for, Onyx."

"I'm thankful to be heard."

While Doc wasn't that much older than most of the people who worked for him, he always fell into a father-figure role with every one of us.

"Listen, I'd like to say this call is a social one, but it isn't."

"What's up?" I asked.

"A couple of things. First, I wanted to alert you that Descanso's sister got ahold of Dutch's cell number. Malin answered and—"

"She just left."

"The sister?"

"That's right."

"Malin feels horrible, and while she said it isn't an excuse, her and Dutch's baby boy is teething and she hasn't gotten much sleep. Since I know how that is, I told her I'd call on her behalf and extend her apologies."

"Tell her I accept."

"Thanks, Onyx. That's mighty understanding of you."

"What's the other thing?"

"It's related. I received a call from Money McTiernan a few minutes ago."

"How is Money liking his new position?" I didn't know the guy well but had been relieved to hear someone K19 worked with regularly had been named the most recent CIA director. There sure as hell had been a string of corrupt directors preceding him.

"Given he's intercepting intel on Thanksgiving, I'm not sure he'd say he's enjoying it. Anyway, that's the primary purpose for this call. He has reason to believe someone is looking for the sister."

"Someone was."

"What do you mean?"

"My cousin Gabe called before she left, saying someone showed up asking for her. She's staying in one of the cottages they rent out to travelers. Anyway, the call left her rattled."

"Interesting. What did Brix tell her?"

"Not exactly sure."

"No worries, Onyx. I'll get in touch with him myself."

Until he called my cousin by his nickname, I'd forgotten how well he and Doc knew one another.

"What about Money? Does he know who or why?" I asked.

"Negative, other than she may be in danger. I'll give Brix a heads-up about that too."

"What kind of danger?"

"Like I said, Money didn't have a lot of details. Let me talk to your cousin, see what I can find out, and then I'll get back to you. We may need to facilitate a relocation. At least temporarily."

"I can tell you where she's headed when she leaves the Central Coast."

"Yeah?"

"The Adirondacks. Same place Ranger's camp is."

"Why?"

"Her family has a cabin on the same lake. It's a place she and her sister used to go when they were kids."

"What's she like?"

If the subject matter wasn't so serious, I would've laughed. Doc was as big a gossip as any of the rest of us were. Women got a bad rap for it, but men were as prone to it. Instead, I took a deep breath and let it out slowly. "They're identical twins, but otherwise, she's nothing like her sister."

"Damn, Onyx. How long was she there?"

"Long enough for me to know."

I thought about what I'd said to Doc quite a while after our call ended. How could I be so sure about Blanca when I'd been so far off the mark with her sister?

Because I'd ignored my instincts. I saw that now. Corazón was hot as fuck. So was her sister. Sex with her had been the best I had in my life. I shook my head. *Sexpionage* was a real thing, and Sofia Descanso had been a pro at it.

I closed my eyes, and instead of picturing Sofia, it was Blanca's face I saw, remembering that when she sat beside me during dinner, I stared into the warmth of her eyes and realized how different they were from her sister's shallow, cold ones.

If I allowed myself to replay my relationship with the woman who'd tried to kill me, I could think of at least a dozen instances when something about her seemed off. I'd ignored it each time, and if that wasn't cause for me to find a new career, nothing would be.

Not that I had a choice. According to the doctors, the chance I would be cleared to fly again had worse odds than being struck by lightning. I remembered the day my orthopedic surgeon had used those very words. At the time, all I could think was that I had already been struck by lightning strong enough to kill me—the wrath of Corazón's storm.

"Where are you staying tonight, bro?" my second-oldest brother, Javier, asked.

"Same as last night." One of my other bosses at K19 Security Solutions, Razor Sharp, had offered me the use of his place when he heard I was planning to spend Thanksgiving on the Central Coast.

"Pretty nice digs," Javi commented.

He was right. The duplex Razor shared with one of the other K19 founding partners, Gunner Godet, sat right on the cliffs overlooking the Pacific Ocean in the seaside village of Cambria, less than a thirty-minute drive from my parents' house.

"You wanna hang out?" I asked.

"Would love to, but I promised my girl I'd rescue her from her family tonight."

"Understood. Have fun." I walked away, feeling more relieved than disappointed. The only company I wanted to keep tonight was my own and that of a bottle of Jack.

Two hours later as I sat alone in Razor's house, I realized how full of shit I was. It wasn't Jack that would ease my pain, no matter how much of it I drank. Somewhere deep in my soul, a voice was trying to tell me what would. Or who. Blanca Descanso. How fucked up was that?

"What?" I barked into my phone a few days later when I grabbed it and answered without looking to see who was calling.

"Onyx. It's Doc."

"Sorry," I said, sitting up in bed and resting my throbbing head in my hand. "What can I do for you?"

"Brix sent footage over from the winery's security cameras, and I forwarded it to Razor."

Razor was known for his uncanny ability to never forget a face. More, he remembered every detail there was to know about the person. He was like a damned computer. "Did he recognize the guy?"

"Yep. Hatchet."

"Fuck," I muttered under my breath when Doc said the name of the notorious hit man. "What's the South End mob want with her?"

"Heard he's freelancing."

If she'd done something to warrant someone putting out a hit on her, maybe my instincts were just as shitty with this Descanso sister as they'd been with the other one.

"Onyx, did you hear me?"

"Sorry, Doc. The call must've cut out."

"Money doesn't think it's a hit. At least not until they find what they're looking for."

"Which is?"

"I don't know definitively, but my guess is Sofia left something behind that may implicate whomever turned her—someone on the inside."

My blood ran cold. "Are you saying you believe there's an agency connection?" Damn, would we ever be able to clear the swamp of corrupt agents and operatives in our own fucking national intelligence agency?

"That is what I'm saying, Onyx. Money thinks so too."

"Which is why he came to you about this rather than keeping it within the CIA."

"Exactly. And the other reason I called you."

"Me? Sorry, Doc, but I'm not cleared for flight. I doubt I will ever be."

"Understood. Which means you need a different kind of assignment."

I looked around the room for the bottle of Jack. It didn't matter if it was still morning—if it was still morning—if Doc wanted to talk about assignments, I needed a drink.

"I'm not ready, sir."

"Bullshit. You're ready, or we wouldn't be talking."

"Yeah, well, I'm telling you I'm not."

"You have fifteen minutes to get yourself together."

What the fuck? "What happens in fifteen minutes?"

"Merrigan and I walk through the front door and brief you on K19's newest unit. The one you're going to head up."

I would've continued to protest, maybe even hung up on the man, if he hadn't beaten me to it.

4

Onyx

"Thanks for the extra five," I said, opening the door after I saw Doc's SUV pull through the duplex's gate and he and his wife, Merrigan "Fatale" Shaw-Butler, get out twenty minutes later rather than fifteen.

"How are you, Onyx?" Merrigan asked, kissing both of my cheeks.

"Not sure I'm as well as your husband thinks I am."

She rested her hand on my arm. "This was my suggestion, not Doc's."

"Please come in," I said after Doc walked up behind her and we embraced.

"Good to have you back in the fold," he said when we took our seats at the dining room table after Merrigan was seated.

She cleared her throat and folded her hands. "All I ask is that you let me finish before making your decision."

Should I tell her it was too late? My mind was made up within seconds of Doc using the word *assignment.*

"K19 Security Solution's profile has risen to where Doc and I believe the covert side of our business has been compromised to the point of ineffectiveness. Given that is where we're needed most, I am proposing a new unit we're referring to as Shadow Ops."

"K19 Shadow Ops?"

"Within K19, yes. To anyone outside, with the exception of Money McTiernan, the unit doesn't exist."

"Who are you tapping?"

"First, you," Merrigan said without cracking a smile.

"And after me?"

"Ranger Messick, Diesel Jacks, and Cowboy Cassidy."

"What's Money's role?"

"Your sole contact within the agency."

"Four men, one with a broken wing, doesn't exactly speak unit to me."

"We have a couple others in mind."

"Who?"

Neither she nor Doc responded.

"Did you or did you not say you wanted me to head this up?"

He tried to hide it, but I caught a glimpse of Doc's grin. "I did."

"Then, I want full transparency. If they're going to be my crew, I want a say in their selection."

Doc didn't bother to mask his smile this time around. "I told you he was ready," he leaned over and said to his wife.

"You didn't, dear husband. I told *you* he was ready."

"Storm Fury and *eventually* Brand Ripa. We'll be looking for your recommendation for others."

"Never heard of the second one."

"Yeah, you have," said Doc. "Brand was—"

"The art forger? Isn't he in prison?"

"Which is why I emphasized the word eventually. I'm working on rehabilitation."

I looked from Doc to Fatale. "Is he serious?"

"We need someone with his expertise," Doc muttered.

I pushed my chair back and walked over to the window. "I knew this had to be a bad dream."

"Brand would serve as a consultant, if you will, until such time as we feel comfortable arranging for his parole."

I spun around. "Let me ask you this. How does AISE feel about his impending release from prison?" He'd only been responsible for the deaths of several of Italy's equivalent of the CIA. It didn't matter that it was inadvertently, except when it came to his trial. I wasn't sure about everything he'd actually been charged with, but it couldn't have been much if Doc was already talking about his parole.

Doc started to respond, but Merrigan held up her hand. "I'll answer that. First, AISE is unaware of the conditions of Brand's incarceration. Second, in order for this new unit to be effective, no one outside of those mentioned previously will be aware of its existence."

"Outside of the current K19 team, you mean."

She shook her head. "Need to know only."

"You mean to tell me Razor, Gunner, and Eighty-eight won't know about it?" The three men I asked about had founded K19 Security Solutions along with Doc before Merrigan was in the picture.

"They have been made aware. Their involvement will remain as needed and very much behind the scenes."

While I was outwardly protesting, I realized I'd already begun formulating a mental list of agents I would like to add to the team.

"This topic of conversation began with me saying you were needed for an assignment."

"That isn't where it began, Doc."

He leaned forward and rested his arms on the table. "No, it isn't. It began when Sofia Descanso shot you."

"What are you asking me to do—specifically?"

"I'm putting you on the sister's detail. You'll have backup from both Ranger and Diesel. More if you need it."

I rolled my neck. "You want me to get close to her."

Merrigan put her hand on my arm. "We all want to know what happened, Onyx. Who got to Sofia, and why were they able to turn her? Doc and I feel personally responsible for every agent, operative, or otherwise that we bring into K19. It was up to us to vet her. We failed, and we want to know where we went wrong, so we don't do it again."

"You think that's the way I see it too, right?"

"Are you saying you don't?"

I shook my head. "Of course I do. How could I not? I was closer to Corazón—Sofia—than anyone."

Shortly before my meeting with Doc and Merrigan ended, his cell phone rang. I was sitting close enough to see the incoming call was from Director McTiernan.

"Money, I've got Merrigan and Onyx here with me. Okay to put the call on speaker?"

"Go ahead."

Doc set the phone on the table.

"Have you read the recent update from Ranger and Diesel?" McTiernan asked.

I raised a brow.

"When I engaged them, I asked them to report their findings both to Money and us," explained Doc before answering Money's question. "I haven't. When did it come in?"

"A few minutes ago. That's why I'm calling. They followed Hatchet to Manhattan." Money hesitated and then added, "Where we've also confirmed Ms. Descanso is presently."

What the hell? "Manhattan? I thought she was headed to a lake in the Adirondacks."

"Evidently, she had a change of plans, Onyx," said Money.

"Do you have anyone else in the area you could engage?" Doc asked.

"That's the thing. I thought you wanted this new team of yours to stay on the down low."

"He's right," said Merrigan. "We need to send in more of our own." She and Doc turned to me.

"I'll engage Wasp and Buster."

I'd flown F/A-18s with Jasper "Wasp" Theron. He'd always been a better pilot than me, not that I would've admitted it before now. Keaton "Buster" Franks was a former Marine Raider—the special forces arm of the USMC.

"What's their twenty?" Doc asked.

"San Luis Obispo." The town was a half hour south of where we were now. It also happened to be where the airfield was located.

"Got anyone who can fly with Wasp?" I knew the question was as hard for Doc to ask as it was for me to answer.

"I heard Swan might be close by, too."

Merrigan put her hand on my arm. "She's good, Onyx."

"I know she is."

Like Wasp, Aubrey Lee was one of the best fighter pilots I'd witnessed fly. She ascended out of the RAF like a damned phoenix, yet her code name, Swan, was far more fitting. She had dark, almost black hair, and steel-blue eyes, but it was her long, graceful neck I'd spent hours daydreaming about sinking my teeth into that was the most exquisite of her features.

I'd always considered her the most beautiful woman I ever laid eyes on—until I met the Descanso sisters.

"Sounds like you're set," said Money, who I'd forgotten was on the line. "I trust you'll engage Ranger and Diesel directly."

"Roger that," I responded before Doc ended the call.

"The Cirrus is fueled and ready at the airfield."

I raised a brow at his offer of the plane's use.

"He has two now," explained Merrigan.

This time, I shook my head. Their price tag, a little over two mil, wasn't as much of a deterrent for anyone who really wanted one as was the scarcity of the planes that made them hard to come by.

Flight time, coast to coast, was a little over five hours. From the airfield in Teterboro, where we were headed, it would take us another fifteen minutes to reach our rendezvous point with Ranger and Diesel—and that was being generous. Our actual flight time in the Blade helicopter was closer to five.

While Swan was with us, she didn't copilot with Wasp. Wasp filled that role when another pilot/agent who was still with the CIA, Trap Flannery, met us in the airfield's terminal and reported Money sent him in to serve as captain. I didn't like McTiernan's interference in a unit that was supposed to be mine to command, especially after he'd commented that, given our desire to keep the team on the down low, he didn't want to send anyone else in from his side.

But I'd known Trap a damn long time, and there was no sense in addressing this now, especially since this was, officially, an agency op. However, we would be evaluating who was responsible for mission planning when this one was complete.

Once we landed and were almost to the heliport where we'd catch the ride on the Blade, Buster reported a message coming in from Ranger.

"He's asking that we go directly to the South Street Seaport. What's there, anyway?"

"Mainly touristy stuff," I answered.

"Think they'll let us land this thing on the Intrepid?" asked Wasp.

I would've laughed, but it was just the kind of thing the crazy asshole would do. The former aircraft carrier served as more of a museum now, and we'd be breaking all sorts of laws by landing on it. Thankfully, Wasp wasn't the one flying the Blade; Trap was.

"There's a heliport due south. Less than half a mile," said Flannery.

Within the few short minutes it took us to arrive at our destination, my cell pinged with a message from Ranger.

"He's reporting that both Descanso and Hatchet have boarded the Circle Line at the Seaport. He and Diesel are getting on now."

How long until departure? I asked via text.

Pulling away from the docks now.

5

Blanca

While it meant driving an extra three hours, I'd arranged to fly into JFK rather than Albany or even Syracuse, which was only ninety minutes from the lake and the camp where I'd spent so many summers with my family.

I hadn't planned to remain in the city, but after spending a few short hours with the man my father believed would one day be my twin's husband, I needed time to get him out of my head before I went to the place where I'd allow my sister to crawl into it.

I saw a Broadway show, wandered around a few museums, took several long walks through Central Park, and today was on a cruise around the island of Manhattan. So far, nothing had managed to keep my thoughts from drifting to Montano. He was with me through it all. Not just in my head; he'd somehow managed to crawl right under my skin.

"First time in New York?" asked the man who sat in the row of empty seats in front of me on the upper deck of the tour boat.

I shook my head.

"A native, then?"

I thought about using my best fluent Italian to tell him I didn't speak English, but decided not to put that much effort into it. "No," I said instead, hoping he'd pick up on the fact that I wasn't interested in conversation. I turned my head and looked out at the landmark the tour's narrator was describing.

"I grew up here but haven't been back for twenty years. Things sure have changed."

The man did have a distinct accent, not that I knew much about the nuances between the boroughs—nor did I care enough—to guess where he was from.

"Take that for example. Yankee Stadium." He pointed to my right. "Five billion dollars to build that thing, and in my opinion, it isn't any better than what was there before."

I didn't point out to him that the narrator had just quoted a price closer to two billion.

"Ever been?" he asked.

"A long time ago."

"See? It was better, right?"

I couldn't believe this jackalope had actually managed to engage me in conversation. I feared now that I'd responded, he wouldn't relent.

"My name's Hatch, by the way. Richard Hatch."

I had no intention of introducing myself, but that didn't seem to matter, given Mr. Chatty was no longer paying the slightest attention to me. Instead, he appeared to be looking at something happening behind the boat. As curious as I was, I stayed seated, even when I saw him rush toward the aft stairwell and down the steps without so much as another glance in my direction. I shrugged, glad to be rid of him.

"Ladies and gentlemen, I'll be taking a break for a few minutes. Kindly stay in your seats as we slow to make our way under the first of seventeen bridges we'll navigate on today's tour."

Until now, the narrator had seemed as unhurried and talkative as the man I'd been glad to see leave. Instead, he seemed equally rushed. Admittedly, I was curious about the abrupt departure of both men, but not enough to leave my seat to investigate. Besides, the bridge we were about to go under seemed close enough to hit my head if I stood.

When the boat slowed to a near crawl, I realized how far off I'd been about how close it was. Still, it was fascinating to look up at the beams of steel and think about the number of cars that had passed over it since it was built so many years ago. It was hard to fathom.

Once safely beyond it, I turned around to take a photo from the opposite side when something attracted my attention. I zoomed in on my phone's camera and snapped a shot of the man standing on the bridge, looking at the back of the boat. The image was still too small for me to see clearly, but at first glance, the man resembled Mr. Chatty.

I was about to turn toward the front when someone else, this time coming up the stairs instead of rushing down, caught my eye.

"What is Montano doing here?" I said out loud even though no one knew him or was close enough to hear me.

Our eyes met, and what stunned me more than anything was that he didn't appear the least bit surprised to see me. Not only that, he was followed by a man who was the spitting image of my first love—Jimmy Messick.

6

Onyx

"Hi, I'm Ranger…err…Owen Messick."

I had to look away when Blanca shook his outstretched hand, her cheeks flushed, and I heard her say, "I could've guessed. You look so much like your brother."

Since I was on her detail for the foreseeable future, I had to figure out a way to get things straight in my head. The woman standing close enough for me to touch was not the woman I'd once believed I was in love with. That woman was dead, and even if she weren't, she was the devil incarnate. *Therefore,* the voice inside my head emphasized, there was no *sane* reason for me to feel possessive of her. Two different minds, bodies, souls, and hearts. Two different people.

I got that. I mean, I didn't think of Blanca as Sofia. I never saw her that way, even mere moments after we met. So why was my inner caveman ready to beat my chest and tell Ranger to keep his hands off her? How could I be so clear and so muddled at the same time?

When I raised my head, both Blanca and Ranger were studying me.

"Sorry, what?"

"I asked why you're here."

"Ranger—Owen—and I were here on business and, when it wrapped early, decided to spend the afternoon as tourists."

"You didn't seem surprised to see me."

"No? I was. I thought you said you were going to the lake."

"I still am, but I wanted to spend a few days in the city first."

"Coincidentally, that's what we're doing."

Ranger slugged my arm "I'm trying to talk this guy into going to the lake instead."

"Oh, uh…wow. Are you?"

I couldn't tell by the look on her face whether she wanted me to or not, but it didn't matter. Wherever she went, I'd follow.

"Gotta admit, being in the mountains is far more my speed than this big city."

"When are you leaving?" Ranger asked Blanca. "Maybe we could carpool.'

She thought about the question for a minute. "I'll have to rent a car. Won't you need one too while you're there?"

"We keep a couple vehicles at the camp."

"Then, sure, I guess."

"When did you say you were leaving?" She hadn't, but I'd much prefer to get her out of the city as soon as possible, even with Wasp and Trap on Hatchet's tail.

"I haven't decided. Maybe tomorrow."

"Perfect. Where are you staying?" I asked even though I already knew.

"A small hotel in Flatiron. You?"

"Same area. At a place called the Mark."

"It's across the street from my hotel."

"Another coincidence. What do you say we meet up for dinner later?"

"We're going to need everyone to take a seat as we go under the next bridge," someone announced over the loudspeaker.

"I'm here," said Blanca, pointing to a chair. I sat beside her and was annoyed as hell when Ranger went around and took the seat next to her on the opposite side.

She inhaled and clasped her shaking hands as we rode under the bridge.

"I bet you could touch it if you stood up," Ranger said to me. At my height, I probably could've.

Blanca laughed. "I thought the same thing. About me, I mean."

When she released her hands and rubbed them on her pant legs, I reached my arm across the back of her chair, barely touching her shoulder with my fingertips. I leaned closer. "Something's bothering you."

Blanca turned her head to look at me, and we were so close I could hear her breathing accelerate. "I'm sure I was imagining things," she said before looking away.

"Tell me what it was."

She shook her head.

"Just tell me."

"There was a man trying to make conversation with me. He left abruptly, and then I swear I saw him standing on the bridge we went under before the last one." Her eyes met mine again. "Crazy, right?"

"Could've been someone who looked like him."

"That's more likely." She pulled out her phone. "I took a photo, but it's grainy."

"Mind if I take a look?"

Her hands were still shaky, so I took the phone from her when she held it up.

"Hard to make out whether it's even a man or a woman," I commented, although I knew exactly who the man on the bridge was. "No need to worry, though." I flexed my other arm. "Ranger and I will protect you." When I smiled, so did she.

"I can see why my sister liked you."

Being on Blanca's detail meant I had to temper my response whenever she mentioned Sofia and particularly my relationship with her, so I did my best not to react. I could tell, though, that it hadn't been enough.

After our boat ride, Blanca, Ranger, and I shared a cab back to our hotels which, as she'd said, were across the street from one another. On the way, I received an update from Wasp, saying he and Trap still had their eyes on Hatchet and his current twenty was in Essex County, at least an hour from where we were.

Since Diesel had swept Blanca's hotel room, placed our own surveillance in it, and was staked out in the one next door, I had no qualms about her heading there on her own.

"How's eight for dinner?" I asked as I walked her into the lobby.

"I'm kind of tired—"

"Seven, then? Or would you like to go earlier?"

She looked at her watch. "It's six now."

"Name the time, and I'll make reservations."

"How about seven thirty?"

"Meet you back here at seven fifteen."

Instead, I arrived at seven and ordered a drink from the bar. The lobby was small, so from where I sat, I could easily see Blanca exit the elevator.

I made use of the time by mentally assessing the team. Ranger and Swan were staked out near the restaurant I'd chosen. Wasp sent another report that Hatchet's twenty hadn't changed, and once Blanca came downstairs and the town car I'd made arrangements for arrived, Buster would be our driver for the evening.

Over dinner, I planned to get Blanca to tell me what Hatchet had said to her, but not at the expense of adding to her anxiety. Since my intention was to spend as much time with her as I could, we'd eventually have that conversation.

I took a sip of my drink and rolled my shoulders. My muscles were stiff from lack of exercise, like they had been when I was at my parents' place. Once we got to the lake, I had to get back into my regular routine, or I'd wind up in too much pain to be helpful if Blanca was in danger.

I heard the ding of the elevator, looked up, and saw her take a step out. She faced the street, her back to me, but I had no complaints about the view. The woman, from any direction, was a walking goddess. Her long dark hair had more red highlights in it than Sofia's had and hung down her back in soft curls that made me want to weave my fingers in them.

The way her white dress clung to her full, round, perky ass made me want to cup those perfect cheeks with my palms. She spun around on her stiletto heels and smiled when she saw me studying her.

I stood and walked in her direction, holding out my hand when we were close enough that she could take it.

"You're stunning."

"Thank you." Her cheeks, pink from spending the afternoon in the sun and on the water, grew more so, and her beautiful smile spread across her face.

The halter-style dress she wore made her already bigger-than-average breasts look even larger. It was all

I could do not to tear my gaze from hers and look down at them.

"Ready?" I asked when I saw Buster pull up out front.

She looked around the bar area. "Where's Ranger?"

"He won't be joining us."

"Oh."

Was that disappointment I heard in her voice? Was her only reason for getting so dolled up to impress him? It sure as hell wouldn't have been for me, now would it? As far as Blanca was concerned, I was her dead sister's boyfriend.

"I'll do my best to be a worthy second choice as your dinner companion," I said, winking through my discomfort.

"Second choice? Um, no, that isn't what I meant. I just…"

"It's okay. I understand. He reminds you of his brother, Jimmy."

Blanca laughed and put her arm through mine. "That isn't what I meant either, but it doesn't matter."

We'd been in the town car for several minutes, me studying her while her focus was on the views we passed by.

"I'm surprised you didn't ask where we were going."

"Hmm?" She turned toward me. "I'm sure wherever you've chosen will be lovely."

If they didn't look so much alike, I would've questioned whether Blanca and Sofia were even related. The twin seated beside me wasn't just warmer, calmer, more alluring; she possessed a grace I hadn't witnessed in her sister.

"What took you to Europe?"

She sat against the seat and looked down at her hands. "It was the farthest place from home I could come up with at the time."

"Where specifically?"

"Italy. I must've watched *Under the Tuscan Sun* thirty times when I was a teenager. I was obsessed."

"Is that where you stayed the whole time you were over there?"

"For the most part. I traveled around quite a bit for my work."

"Which is?"

Her cheeks flushed again. "I'm a writer."

"What do you write?"

Blanca turned her head toward the window. "Fiction, mainly."

"You gonna make me drag it out of you, sis?"

"It isn't that interesting, honestly."

I leaned closer. "Let me guess. You write that *Fifty Shades* stuff?"

"Not quite."

"Okay. You don't want to tell me now. I'll get it out of you later." I rested my hand on the seat between us like hers was and brushed her pinky with mine. "Just joshing. I'll stop buggin' you."

"It's a little racier than that."

"Wait. What? It's racier?"

Blanca raised her chin. "Yes."

"Well, damn, sis. Can I read it?"

She laughed out loud, and, wow, it was a beautiful sound. "Maybe someday.'

"You write under a pseudonym or your own name?"

"I'll never tell."

"Damn, girl…" What? What could I say to her? I wish I'd known you before your twin because I think you're the prettiest, smartest, sexiest woman I've ever met? Fuck. This was a major Charlie Foxtrot, if there ever was one.

"Are you okay?"

"Yep. Fine and dandy. Hey, if you loved Italy, then I think you're going to enjoy where we're having dinner."

When we pulled up to the most exclusive hardest-to-snag-a-reservation-at restaurant in all of New York City, Blanca's mouth dropped open.

"You're kidding. We aren't really eating here."

"Sure, we are."

"Why? How?"

The owner of the restaurant was someone I used to pilot for occasionally. Since I had no intention of telling Blanca why I wouldn't be returning to that particular career, I kept my answer simple. "I know a guy."

The food was amazing. I was sure of it. Not that I remembered a thing about it. I could, however, remember every word Blanca uttered, every smile, and every nuance in the way she angled her neck and leaned in whenever I spoke.

Instead of talking about my job—present or former were both off-limits—I told her about growing up in California and all the trouble my brothers and I used to get into.

Blanca didn't say much about Sofia, probably for the same reason I didn't talk about work, but somehow, the conversation never stopped.

I did a double take on the time I read on my watch, incredulous that it was almost eleven.

"I've kept you up past your bedtime," I said when she pushed the crème brûlée we'd shared toward me and I took the last bite.

"What would you say if I told you I wasn't ready for our night to end?"

7

Blanca

As soon as I said the words, I realized what they implied. My statement was accurate; I wasn't ready for our night to end. I'd never enjoyed conversation with anyone as much as I did with Montano. He was intelligent, witty, attentive, and flirted just enough that it buoyed my ego without it feeling as though he was coming on to me.

"I have an idea."

I tried my hardest not to cringe in anticipation of what he might suggest. He reached over and covered my hand with his.

"Don't worry, sis. I know what you meant."

His continual use of the word sis should relieve me, but it didn't. I was ashamed to admit it, even to myself, but I didn't want him to think of me that way. I wanted him to want me as a woman in the same way he'd wanted my sister. What kind of person did that make me? A horrible one.

He squeezed my fingers. "Hey, what's wrong?"

"I don't want you to think I'm…"

"Being friendly? Getting to know me like I'm getting to know you?"

Of course Montano would make me feel at ease. Hadn't he been all evening?

He released my fingers but kept his hand on mine. "I say we ask the driver waiting out front to take us for a drive through Central Park."

"I'd really like that."

He stood, helped me with my chair, and as we exited the restaurant, kept his hand on the small of my back.

When we got in the car, he sat close enough that our arms brushed against each other. As tall as he was, when he adjusted his long legs, our thighs touched too.

Perhaps it was the wine we'd shared at dinner that went straight to my head, but with our bodies rubbing against each other's, I had to squeeze my thighs together to ease my ache of want.

"I hope you don't want to take off too early tomorrow," he said a few minutes later when we were on the road that cut through the park.

"I don't, but why?"

"Since the weather is so nice, I'd like to go for a run here in the morning."

"Me too."

He nudged me, kind of like you might see a kid do to another kid. "It's a date, then."

When I yawned twice in close proximity, Montano asked the driver to take us back to our hotel. Not hotel—hotels. He was the perfect gentleman and walked me inside and over to the elevator.

"I had a nice time tonight," he said, leaning forward to kiss my cheek.

"I did too. Thank you again for dinner. It was fabulous and very extravagant." Not that I saw a bill. Considering no one stopped us on the way out, he must've made prior arrangements to pay it.

"It was my pleasure."

"Well, good night, then." I stepped inside the elevator, raising my hand to my cheek where he'd kissed me once the doors closed.

Before we exited the town car, we'd made arrangements to meet at eight the following day to go for our run. I wondered, as I tossed and turned, unable to sleep, if Ranger would join us. I hoped not.

When I exited the elevator fifteen minutes early the next morning to get a coffee before we left, Montano was already in the lobby, waiting for me.

"Did I get the time wrong?" I asked.

"Not at all." He reached behind him and held up two cups. "One straight-up black coffee. One skim latte. Which would you prefer? Or would you like something else?"

"Which do you prefer?"

He smiled. "I drink it both ways."

"Latte, please."

"I thought that's what you'd pick."

"Will Ranger be joining us this morning?"

I caught a quick glimpse of a frown before Montano said, "He's still asleep." He reached into his pocket. "You want me to wake him up and tell him to get his ass over here?" His cheeks pinkened. "Sorry for my language."

I laughed. "First of all, remember what kind of books I write. Second, no, I was hoping it would just be the two of us."

He put his phone away and leaned against the bar behind him. "You do my ego good."

"I doubt your ego suffers much, Montano."

The smile left his face. "You'd be surprised."

Since he didn't elaborate, I assumed he didn't want to talk about it. I finished my coffee and tossed the cup in the recycle bin. "Ready?"

"When you are."

As we exited the front door of the hotel, I saw the same town car and driver waiting out front. "Did he sleep here?"

"Nah, I'm not that mean. I did tell him to get here by seven, though."

"Why?"

"In case you came downstairs early."

I waited while the driver got out and opened the back door of the car.

"You're always anticipating the needs of others, aren't you?"

"You met my mama. She'd get after me if she heard I wasn't a gentleman."

"It's more than that," I murmured when he waved me into the car.

The driver said he'd be on standby and when we finished our run, to just send him a text.

"Doesn't that get expensive?"

"Nah. He gives me a discount."

"Someone you know, then?"

"An acquaintance."

We ran the trails of Central Park, occasionally stopping to take in the scenery. Most of the trees had lost their leaves, but there were still some exhibiting their rich fall colors. At one point, I noticed a rowboat out on the lake. In it were two older people. The man was paddling slowly, while the woman held an umbrella to shield them both from the sun.

"Do you mind?" I asked, pulling out my phone to take a photo.

"Not at all."

I snapped several and put my phone away.

"Why them?"

"What do you mean?"

Montano waved his hand in the direction of the lake. "While there aren't many people out, there are some. Why did you only take a photo of that couple?"

I shrugged. "Inspiration."

"For your books?" He raised a brow, perhaps due to their age.

"It isn't all sex. There's a story there too. A happily ever after, if you will."

"You believe in that?"

I thought about the question as we ran. "I suppose I do, since I write it."

"You want that for yourself?"

"Doesn't everyone?" I asked.

"I guess."

"Sometimes, it's hard to believe it will happen."

He nodded but didn't speak again for several minutes.

When we came around a bend and saw two people seated on a bench, each playing a cello, we stopped to listen. I pulled my phone out and took a short video of them.

"More inspiration?" Montano asked.

"Maybe."

"Let me see if I can piece it together. This is the couple from the boat. They met at Julliard and came to the park to practice every day. Soon, they fell in love. Now, they've given up playing but come to the park, and he rows her around the lake."

"Wow. You're good. Maybe you should be the one to write their story."

He'd been smiling, but stopped. "I wouldn't be any good at writing the happy ending."

I watched as he turned and picked up our run, wondering what made someone who could see the same story I did so clearly, think there couldn't be a happy ending.

8

Onyx

Chump. That should be my code name. Hadn't I learned my lesson from Sofia? Now, here I was, imagining the same happy ending I thought she and I would have, with her *twin* sister.

Just like I said last night, Blanca was being friendly. That's it. What was it about me—and the twin sisters—that made me so ready to jump to the happily-ever-after part? I wasn't such an idiot with any other women. Never had been. Not in my whole life. So why them? Did magical blood flow through their veins?

"Hey, Montano!" I heard Blanca call after me. When I turned around, she was pointing to another pathway. I ran back in her direction to see what had caught her attention. Another group was set up in the park, playing music, except instead of a duo, this was six guys playing jazz.

Like she had earlier, Blanca pulled out her phone and took a short video. "They're really good, right?"

They were. In fact, I wondered if they played any clubs or even larger venues. Also like she had with the couple playing cellos, she pulled out some cash and tossed it into their collection basket. I hadn't paid attention before, but this time I saw she gave them two twenties. Maybe more.

"Generous," I commented when we resumed our run.

"It's the least I can do."

"Why do you say that?"

"Their inspiration is invaluable."

"Yeah? You gonna write them into your next book?"

"Of course I am."

When we came to the edge of the park, I saw Buster waiting with the car.

"Wow," mumbled Blanca, noticing him like I had. "Has he got a tracker on you or something?"

I laughed, and so did she, but the truth was, he had one on both of us.

A little under two hours later, Blanca had picked up her rental car and we were on our way to the Adirondacks. I was relieved when Buster drove Ranger, her, and me to the rental place and I saw she'd reserved a full-size SUV. If she'd gotten a compact instead, I would've had to rent my own car. Either that or not been able to walk upon arrival after sitting in a cramped position for four hours.

The drive north was breathtaking. It was surprising, the number of people who believed all of the state was just like Manhattan. Nothing could be further from the truth. The majority of it was rural, with rolling green hills, farms, and historic towns and villages.

"It's a bit of a side trip, but I've always wanted to see the Baseball Hall of Fame," said Blanca when we were nearing the turnoff that would take us to Cooperstown.

I looked over my shoulder at Ranger.

"I've been a bunch, but I'm in," he said, looking at something on his phone.

"I'm in too. I've never been."

Blanca pulled up in front of the historic building. "I always wondered why they built it here. Especially since it isn't near a major league ballpark."

"Right there is where the game of baseball started." Ranger pointed at a well-maintained field across the street.

"That makes sense."

"Took them quite a while to prove it, though."

We spent two hours taking our time, wandering through the various galleries. Watching Blanca study each of the exhibits made me wonder if she'd write this into her next book too.

"Mind if we get something to eat before we get back on the road?" I asked, rubbing my stomach as we were leaving.

"It's Friday," said Blanca. "And you know what that means!"

I shrugged.

"Fish fry!" she and Ranger shouted at the same time.

Feeling like a third wheel, I held back as they raced down the block to the tavern on the corner. I took the opportunity to check my cell for messages.

Hatchet is on the move but headed in the opposite direction, said a text from Wasp.

Where to? I responded.

Almost to Atlantic City.

That a guy connected to the South End mob was headed there, wasn't a big surprise. However, it meant we needed to be on the lookout for his replacement.

I alerted Buster before going in and joining Blanca and Ranger, whom I found sitting at the bar.

"Genny Cream Ale is the best," I heard her say before clinking her bottle with his.

I had never been an insecure guy, and thus, jealousy wasn't in my nature, but since Blanca and Ranger had met on the tour boat, I was certainly feeling it.

"I wasn't sure if you'd want one," said Blanca when I came to stand behind the two of them.

"Hey, I'm all in. Fried fish, beer, bring it on."

"Fish fry." When Ranger corrected me, I felt like knocking him off his damned bar stool. Instead, I shot him a glare.

"When's the last time you checked in with the office?"

His face dropped, and he stood. "You're right. Better do that. Excuse me."

"I'm a spoilsport."

"No, you're not." Blanca signaled the bartender and pointed at me. "What I'm having," she told him.

"So tell me, what's so great about *fish fry*?"

"It's just a thing. I guess the real story is that a priest in a village with equal numbers of parishioners who raised cattle and who made money from commercial fishing declared it would be a sin to eat meat on Fridays, thus boosting the fishermen's sales."

"No one caught on?"

"I guess so, but not for many years."

"Are you religious?"

"I believe in God, if that's what you're asking. I sometimes eat meat on Fridays, and I can't remember the last time I was in a church other than for my father's funeral."

I could say the same, although when that plane was going down, I'd prayed every second. Once I woke up from the coma too. However, then, there were just as many times I prayed God would end my misery.

"I'm sorry."

I looked into Blanca's eyes. "What for?"

"Sometimes I say the wrong thing. A lot of times, I feel like I do with you."

"What makes you think that?"

She reached out as if she was about to touch my cheek, but pulled back. "You have the kindest, sweetest face. And then I say the wrong thing, and it changes so drastically."

"That isn't on you, sis."

"Can I get you another?" the bartender asked her.

"Please." When he walked away, she added, "If I weren't driving, I'd have a shot too."

"What's your go-to?"

"Irish whiskey."

"Damn, girl."

"I know, it's terrible, right?"

"Hell, no. It's my go-to too. Don't forget you put Ranger and me on as drivers. We'll make him drive."

"He won't mind?"

"Don't care if he does. I'm his boss."

I ordered the shots, another beer for myself, and a glass of water for Ranger, who still hadn't returned. I hoped it didn't mean bad news.

"Back to the fish. What's so great?"

"First, they bring you a piece of beer-battered fish that's this long."

When she held her hands about a foot apart, I rolled my eyes.

"I'm serious. And if it's a real fish fry, it comes with German potato salad, coleslaw, and a roll."

"And if it isn't real?"

"They'll try to substitute regular potato salad or even macaroni salad." Blanca grimaced.

"What about this place? Real or fake?"

"Real all the way. Look." She pointed to the description on the menu, and sure enough, the dinner came with German potato salad and coleslaw.

Ranger came in from outside and eyed our empty shot glasses.

"You're our DD," I told him.

He laughed. "Of course I am."

"Hope you don't mind," said Blanca, taking a swig of her beer.

"And if I did?"

"Guess you'd be crap out of luck since Montano is your boss."

When they brought our plates to us at the bar, I was stunned to see Blanca wasn't exaggerating about the size of the piece of fish. Even as big as it was, I wanted a second helping.

When Ranger excused himself to the restroom, I leaned back on the stool and rubbed my belly. "You weren't kidding about how good that was."

"Stick with me, and who knows what other secret delights you'll discover."

There was no question, like last night, that she regretted the words as soon as she said them. Fueled by a second shot and a beer, I leaned forward, so tempted to have a taste of her lips. I didn't, though. I also didn't tell her the kind of secret delights I wished she'd show me.

She sat back in her chair, putting more distance between us. "Sorry. That came out wrong."

"Did it?"

She nodded.

"You sure?"

She got up from the bar and turned in the direction Ranger had gone, but I grabbed her wrist. "Tell me if you're sure, Blanca?"

"As sure as you are."

9

Blanca

I wasn't just playing with fire; I'd ignited the equivalent of a stick of dynamite, and it was about to blow up in my face.

Secret delights? God, what had I been thinking? I hadn't been. That was the problem. Ever since Montano had answered so quickly and emphatically that he and my sister would not have ended up married, somewhere in the back of my mind, I saw him as fair game, convincing myself the two were nowhere near as close as my father had made them out to be.

I shook my head hard, trying to get the image of him and my sister out of my head.

Why him, dammit? Why was the first man I was really, truly, wildly attracted to, my sister's ex? I looked up at the ceiling and raised my fist. "How could you do this to me?" I said out loud, not knowing if I was talking to God or Sofia or both.

I looked in the mirror of the ladies' room, my eyes filled with tears, and I splashed cold water on my face.

Maybe what I needed was to sober up. I turned my head when I heard the door opening. I went to grab a paper towel at the same moment someone grabbed my arm and spun me around to face him.

"I'm not going to apologize for this, before or after," Montano growled right before crashing his lips into mine. Without thinking, I wrapped my arms around his neck and opened my mouth to his.

God, he could kiss. He must've had a third shot before following me into the ladies' room; he tasted of Irish whiskey chased with my favorite beer.

His hands eased down to my ass, and I ground myself against him. Was I wanton? Damn right, I was. If it weren't the middle of the afternoon and we weren't in the restroom of a tavern, I'd cup the hardness I could feel pressing against me and beg him to fuck me.

When I weaved and he steadied me, I realized exactly how intoxicated I was. "Montano," I groaned.

He kissed me once more before abruptly pulling away. "I told you I wouldn't apologize." He stalked out of the ladies' room, leaving me scratching my head.

I rested my hands on the edge of the sink, trying to clear my muddled brain. It was foggy before, but after that kiss—*oh my God.*

What was I supposed to do now? How would I face him? Not just him. How would I face Ranger? We still had at least an hour's drive ahead of us. I mean, I could sit in the back seat, behind Montano, so he couldn't see me.

I stood up straight, squared my shoulders, and walked back out to the bar. Ranger was there, but there was no sign of the man who had just kissed the shit out of me. I grasped the back of the nearest stool when I felt myself weave a little.

"Are you okay?" asked Ranger, walking over to where I still stood.

"Fine. Just a little dizzy."

"Are you ready to go?"

"Where's your compatriot?"

"At the car. Said he needed some air, so I volunteered to wait here for you."

"That was nice. Thank you."

When Ranger held out his arm, I took it, still feeling a little unsteady on my feet.

As we walked down the block, I didn't see Montano waiting by the car. Maybe he needed a lot of air after that kiss. Or maybe he was regretting it. But he said he wouldn't apologize. That wasn't exactly the same thing as regret, though, now was it?

Ranger stepped forward to open the front passenger door for me.

"I can sit in the back," I offered.

"Too late," he said, pointing over the seat to where Montano was stretched out—as much as someone of his height and stature could be—evidently out cold, given the volume of his snoring.

Ranger laughed. "Onyx isn't very good at holding his liquor. In fact, he usually limits himself to one. I've never seen him do a shot."

"Onyx?"

"Nickname," he muttered, closing the door behind me after I climbed inside.

"Can't believe what a small world it is," said Ranger, pulling into the driveway that sat between his family's camp and mine. I got out as soon as he cut the engine and checked out the cabin I hadn't seen in over a decade.

It didn't look much different than it had years ago. The porch hadn't been swept, and the furniture that usually crowded the small space was probably stored in the basement. I wondered how long it had been since my dad was up here as I reached inside the secret door that looked like it was part of the siding but was the place we always put the key to the front door.

"I can get those," I said to Ranger, who brought my bags up the porch steps.

"I got it."

The air was oppressive as I pushed open the door and stepped inside.

"Needs a good airing out," he said, still holding my bags. "Where would you like these?"

I'd always slept in the loft upstairs instead of the bedroom on the main floor, but I wouldn't feel comfortable doing so now. "In there," I said, pointing at the door right off the kitchen.

"I don't remember ever being inside this place."

"No?" I responded absentmindedly as I walked around, opening what windows I could. Many of them were stuck.

"Need some help?" asked Ranger.

I stepped aside, and he pushed one open with what looked like one finger.

"I loosened it for you," I joked.

"Don't emasculate me, woman."

"Am I interrupting?" Montano said from just inside the doorway.

"Not at all," answered Ranger. "If you're done catching up with your beauty sleep, we could use some help."

"Let me get that." I stepped aside to let Montano open another window I was struggling with. "Sorry, I zonked out on you, sis."

"Lightweight," Ranger said with a cough.

Montano glared at him.

"If you don't need my help, I, uh, better go get my place opened up."

"Don't you worry. I got this, son," Montano answered.

"If you want to finish down here, I'll get started upstairs," I said, rushing up the old wooden steps. Seconds later, I heard heavy footsteps behind me.

"You runnin' from me, Blanca?" he called after me.

"I just want to get the camp aired out."

"I'm curious. Why do you and Ranger keep calling these places camps? Why not cabins?"

"It started back in the early eighteen hundreds. No one really vacationed in the Adirondack mountains before then. It was only after the railroad built a route from Saratoga Springs, which is east of here, up to the north of Lake George, that there was a way for anyone to even get here." This was a story I'd heard my father tell so many times that I recited it by rote. "Sorry, this is boring."

"Not at all. Keep going."

"Well, once the line was established, developers started building hotels. Pretty soon, there were more than two hundred, but what those developers learned was that tourists wanted a more authentic camping experience. So, the owners of the hotels cleared areas for simple tent camps. From there, they built lean-tos, which eventually became compounds of rustic cabins. What probably started out as a marketing ploy, stuck. You'll rarely hear anyone refer to the cabins or cottages as anything but a camp. Unless they aren't from here, of course."

"Like me."

"You get used to it," I said, trying with all my might to get the last window open.

"I got this," Montano said to me like he'd said to Ranger.

"I can't forget to come back upstairs and close them later. It's going to get chilly right around four in the afternoon."

He looked around the loft at the six beds that occupied the space. "Everybody just slept up here in one room?"

"Mainly just the kids. We'd take turns going to the different camps. The parents probably arranged it so they'd get a break at least once during the week. It was a giant slumber party."

"Were these parties co-ed?" he asked with wide eyes.

I shook my head. "The boys had to sleep on one side of the loft and the girls on the other."

"And no one ever sneaked over to the other side?"

I knew my cheeks had turned bright red, remembering when Jimmy Messick did just that and how my father somehow knew and was upstairs in a flash. Jimmy got sent home that night and was never allowed at another slumber party at our camp.

"What?" I asked, looking up at Montano, who was studying me.

"You gonna tell me the story or keep it all to yourself?"

"It isn't that interesting, I promise." I sat down on the floor with my back against one of the beds. "We sure had a lot of fun here, though."

He wiggled his eyebrows.

"*Innocent* fun."

"What was your favorite thing to do when you were here?" he asked.

"It would be hard to name just one, but if I had to, I would say it was the nights we all sat around the table and played cards. We'd play Crazy Eights for nickels and just laugh and laugh."

While the memory was one of my best, as soon as the words left my mouth, a chill coursed through my body. It was almost as if I sensed danger present, and I knew I had to get out of the camp. "Excuse me," I said, using my arms to push myself up. I raced down the stairs, but the feeling persisted, so I went outside and down to the dock. Even then, the feeling remained.

10

Onyx

As I followed Blanca out of the cabin, I sent a message to Ranger. I'd watched as her expression changed. Something had spooked her, and her instincts told her to get out. It was the same thing everyone who'd gone through the kind of training I had, had drummed into them. *If in doubt, get out.*

"What happened in there?" I asked.

Her arms were wrapped tightly around her waist. "I don't know. Maybe a panic attack."

"Do you feel better now that you're outside?"

"Not really."

I pulled one arm away from her body and grasped her hand. "Come with me."

"Where are we going?" she asked when I approached the SUV we'd arrived in.

"Somewhere else." I backed out of the driveway and went in the direction of the bridge I remembered from my last time here. "Is that amusement park this way?" I asked.

"If it's still there, yes."

A couple of miles down the road, we could see the place in the distance. "It doesn't look as big as it used to be, or open," said Blanca.

"You're right, and, damn, I wanted one of those soft-serve ice cream cones."

"That does sound good."

"What was your favorite, chocolate or vanilla?"

"Vanilla dipped in chocolate."

I rubbed my belly. "Damn, girl, you sure are teasing me."

Blanca gave me a tight smile, but it didn't shine through her eyes. Like her sister's, they looked shallow and cold.

I reached over and covered her hand with mine. "Come on back to me, Blanca."

She raised her brows. "What do you mean?"

I squeezed her fingers. "Give me a real smile."

"That was—"

"No, it wasn't." She cocked her head, looked into my eyes, and this time when she smiled, the warmth was back. "There it is." Out of habit, I guess, I brought her hand to my lips and kissed it.

"Montano…"

"Shh." I kissed the back of her hand a second time before letting go.

"Hey, look! It's open!" she exclaimed. While the rest of the amusement park looked like it had been closed for years, the ice cream stand had a line out front.

I parked the SUV, and before I could come around to open her door, Blanca was almost to the back of the queue.

"Sorry," she said when I joined her, "I got nervous when I saw that." She pointed to where a school bus pulled up. As soon as the door opened, thirty or more kids raced over and got in line behind us.

"Good call, sis."

"I'm so sad the carousel is boarded up," Blanca said after we got our ice cream and walked what I assumed was once a bustling midway. "It was so beautiful."

"Come with me." I pulled her over to the side of the building where I'd noticed a window. "Hold this," I said, handing her my cone.

"What are you—"

I circled her waist and lifted her into the air. "Can you see it?"

"Oh, yes. And it's more spectacular than I remembered."

I looked up, more to get another glimpse of her smile than anything else, but caught her taking a lick of my cone. "Hey, what do you think you're doing!" I squeezed her waist.

Blanca giggled. "It was going to drip."

"Sure, it was." As I slid the back of her body down the front of mine, I leaned over her shoulder and took a big bite of her ice cream.

"Hey!" she shouted, giggling even more.

"Turn around is fair play, sis."

When I set her on her feet, the smile left her face.

"I'm sorry. It's just a habit. I won't do it anymore."

"That isn't it." When I let go completely, she walked toward the lake.

"What is it, then?"

She walked out on a dock and sat down, hanging her legs over the side. "I don't want to tell you."

"Come on, spill."

Blanca shook her head. "It'll make me sound like the most awful person."

"Since I already know you're not, go ahead." I had to bite my tongue to stop from telling her that her sister was the awful one.

"Is this what it was like? You know, between you and Sofia?"

I sat beside her and leaned back on my hands. "Um, yeah, we had fun…"

"But?"

"It wasn't like this."

"What do you mean?"

I tucked a strand of her hair behind her ear. "It wasn't like this," I repeated, grappling to find the right words without divulging too much about her twin.

"It was better, right?" She squeezed her eyes closed. "Why am I asking questions I don't want answers to?"

"It wasn't ever this good."

"The fact that what you just said makes me happy means I'm a worse person."

I shook my head. "Not even a little."

She leaned on her hands like I was. "The last thing I said to my sister was that I hated her."

Ironic that the last words I'd said were that I loved her. "Bad fight?" I sure had experienced enough of those with my own siblings.

"It was more than that. I mean, I'm sure she was very different by the time you met her, but the Sofia I grew up with wasn't a very nice person."

"Is that why you left?"

"They say parents don't have favorites, but in our family, they did. I was always a mama's girl, while in my dad's eyes, my twin could do no wrong. Once my mom died, I didn't feel like I belonged anymore."

"So you ran away and never came back?"

"Something like that."

"What happened back at the cab…camp?"

"I can't explain it. It was as though a chill descended on me, and I knew I had to get out of there."

"What about now?"

"I'm good." She shuddered. "I know we have to go back, but I'm not in any hurry."

"Neither am I."

"Ouch!" she shrieked, pulling her feet out of the water. "Those little bastards bit my toes."

I checked out her perfectly pedicured toes with the bright-orange nail polish and envied the fish who'd nibbled on them. "Let me see if they broke the skin," I said, pulling her legs onto my lap when she turned sideways. When I didn't see any sign of blood, I massaged her soles.

"Oh my God, that feels amazing." She lay back on the dock and rested her arm over her eyes. I moved from her feet to her ankles and then up her calves, kneading her flesh as I went. "You are really good at that," she moaned with a breathy sexiness to her voice that sent a current of desire straight to my groin.

Fortunately, the highest I could go was where her pant legs were rolled up to her knees. I gave her leg a squeeze before letting go.

"Thanks," she said, sitting up, but not putting her feet back in the water. "I can't believe how warm it is, given it's the beginning of December."

"Ranger mentioned there's a snowstorm on its way."

Blanca's eyes opened wide. "I should probably think about getting some provisions, then. Unless…"

I looked at her with a raised brow. "Are you thinking about leaving?"

She shrugged one shoulder. "There's something I need to find first, and I haven't even started looking. Once I've done that, my plan is to fix it up and put the camp on the market."

"What are you looking for?"

"That's the thing. I don't know exactly."

"Maybe I could help you. You said you didn't know *exactly*. What do you know?"

"Only that my sister left something at the camp for me and it's imperative I find it. That's all my father said."

"Makes it tough with nothing else to go on. Do you have any guesses about what it might be?"

"She said it might be jewelry. Or maybe something of their mom's," I told Ranger later after Blanca and I got back to the camps after stopping at the market and I'd helped put her groceries away.

"What do you think it is?" he asked.

"Whatever Hatchet was hired to get his hands on."

"My thoughts too. So, what's your plan?"

"How bad is this storm predicted to be?"

"They're saying to expect at least a foot. Maybe as much as three."

11

Onyx
The Night Before Thanksgiving
One Year Ago
Miami

We'd been on standby for seventy-two hours, waiting for the "go" to transport two of K19's contracted operatives to Columbia for an undercover assignment. Landry "Tackle" Sorenson would be placed inside the US Embassy in Bogotá while Knox "Halo" Clarkson would infiltrate one of the South American country's drug cartels.

I wasn't sure how the hell Halo had been assigned such a high-risk mission, given one year ago this week, he and Tackle were undercover in Somalia when they were kidnapped by pirates. I'd been part of the team who went in and rescued them. I'd done my damnedest to get them home to be with their families in time for the holiday, but I just couldn't make it happen.

It was shit luck that the timing of this particular mission coincided with the Thanksgiving holiday once again.

Corazón and I hadn't made any plans to be with her family or mine this year, given the "go" could come at any moment. While I'd met her father before, she'd never met my mother or any of my siblings, a fact she wasn't happy about.

"I can't remember the last time I was with them for Thanksgiving. It isn't a big deal in our family," I'd told her. It wasn't the truth. Not by a long shot. But given my family lived on the West Coast and we were on the opposite side of the country with strict orders to be at the ready, it was impossible for us to leave. That hadn't seemed to either matter or appease her.

We spent a quiet night—only because she wasn't speaking to me—in what she referred to as a "shitty" hotel room; it seemed fine to me. With Corazón, it was always about money, something that was beginning to grate on me.

When the call came in at zero eight hundred the next morning, saying Tackle and Halo were en route, I was in the shower.

"Trap Flannery is waiting for us at the airfield. We need to head out," Corazón added after informing me the order to deploy had come directly from Monk.

Still half asleep, I wondered when Trap had been brought in on the op, but it didn't matter. He was still with the CIA, outranked me, and this was their mission. K19 had only been given the assignment to carry it out.

I thought briefly about contacting Monk Perrin, K19's lead for the mission, or Money McTiernan, who was Monk's primary agency contact. However, today was Thanksgiving. It made sense Money would've tapped someone like Trap as a secondary point person.

I also wondered if he planned to captain the flight over me. Again, as tired and fed up with Corazón's behavior as I was, I really didn't give a shit.

When we arrived at the airfield, Corazón went to talk to Trap first while I fetched our coffee.

"Hey, man, happy Thanksgiving," I said, walking up and shaking his hand.

"Same to you, Onyx. Sucks not being top guy on the totem pole on a holiday, doesn't it?"

I shrugged. "Never big on them anyway." As soon as I'd said the words, I felt bad. While I wasn't, Trap was a family man. From what I remembered, he had at least two kids he was forced to be away from whenever a mission was given a go.

"You flyin' to Bogotá with us this afternoon?"

"Thankfully, no. My job is just to fill in as mission planner on the CIA side to make sure Tackle's and Halo's assignments and identities are firmly in place."

"Copy that."

Corazón and I worked out flight plans, manifests, and instrumentation checks on the aircraft. We hadn't been done long when Trap informed us Tackle and Halo had arrived.

"I'll file the reports with the airfield and copy K19, unless there's something else you want me to do," said Corazón.

If Trap hadn't been within earshot, I would've told her all I really wanted was for her to leave her pissy-ass attitude here in Miami so we could get this mission over with. That, though, might lead to conversations about what would happen once we returned.

I hadn't told her this, but I'd requested a private meeting with the managing partner of K19. All hell would break loose if Corazón got wind of it, especially if she found out the reason for my request was to ask for a reassignment and a different copilot.

It was impossible to know with Corazón, but maybe her quick temper had as much to do with her being sick of spending so much time with me as I was with her.

We'd been in the air two hours when we ran into a full-blown, out-of-the-blue weather system just over Aruba—not uncommon for the area. "What the fuck?" I spat when I tried to gauge our location in relation to the storm and realized both the communication and radar systems were down. "Check the circuits," I told her, trying to gain better control of the aircraft.

"Venezuela's grid is out," said Corazón, looking at something on her phone.

"What are you talking about?"

"That's whose airspace we're in. There's a total blackout."

"Connect with Columbia."

Corazón was still studying her phone.

"Did you hear me? Fucking connect with Columbia. I need to know where to divert."

She glared at me and then manually entered coordinates into the system that rerouted us over Columbia's Macuira National Park.

"Sorry about all that turbulence, guys," I hollered back to Tackle and Halo when we were out of whatever weather system had been tossing and turning our aircraft.

"Maybe you oughta give the stick to Corazón, dude," Tackle hollered back.

"You hear that?" I said, laughing. "You ready to take my stick?"

When I turned to face her, the last thing I expected to see was the woman I'd referred to as my heart for the last several months, pointing a gun at me.

When she cocked it and took aim, I knew that within seconds, I'd be dead. There was only one thing that raced through my mind. "I love you, Corazón," I said to her. She pulled the fucking trigger anyway.

12

Blanca

"Oh no!" I groaned when the electricity suddenly cut out. I peered out the window and saw that Ranger's place was still lit up. Why would my electricity go out and not his?

It was pitch-black since the moon was shrouded by clouds and it couldn't be more than ten degrees outside, so there was no way I was going to try to make my way outside and to the basement to see if a circuit blew.

On the other hand, it would quickly become too cold to stay in the camp unless the power came back on in the next few minutes.

I jumped and put my hand on my heart when I heard someone pounding on the front door. "Blanca, are you in there?" A flashlight shone in the window.

"Coming," I shouted at Montano, feeling my way from the kitchen to the entryway. "The power's out," I said, stating the obvious and letting him in.

"Where's your breaker?" he asked.

"In the cellar."

"We'll have to wait until tomorrow to dig our way through the snow to get to it. Why don't you get whatever you need to stay next door tonight?"

"Are you sure I won't be an imposition?"

"Where else you gonna go, sis?"

"Right. Um, thanks."

Montano led the way to the bedroom off the kitchen, where I tossed a few things into a bag. He carried it for me while I put on a jacket and the only pair of boots I'd brought, which wouldn't do much good in the snow since they were ankle height. "I'll grab some stuff from the bathroom on the way out since it's by the front door."

As soon as we stepped out onto the porch, Montano dropped my bag and swept me into his arms.

"What are you doing?"

"Snow's too deep. I'll come back for your stuff."

"I can walk," I protested, even though I knew he was right. My boots were useless.

He shook his head and trudged the distance between the two camps. Once next door, he set me down and returned for my stuff.

"Come on in," said Ranger, holding the door open for me.

"Sorry about this."

"No need to apologize. Your place was never winterized. We have two backup generators over here."

"Your power went out too?"

"Yes, ma'am."

I shook my head, wondering what in the world I thought I was doing. I should leave as soon as the snow cleared and catch the next plane back to Italy. I could hire someone to sell the camp. While I was curious about whatever I was supposed to find, I didn't share my father's opinion that doing so was "imperative."

"How about a hot toddy?"

"I'll take one," said Montano, coming inside with my bag. "Let me get your coat."

"Thanks, and yes, please," I said, looking from him to Ranger.

"Oh, I should tell you that Onyx's version of the drink is hot chocolate with butterscotch. Mine is with peppermint schnapps."

"That sounds a lot better than hot Irish whiskey. I'll take butterscotch please."

"See, son? I told you butterscotch is the ticket. Everybody likes it better than peppermint."

"Everybody but me," muttered Ranger, walking away.

"Come sit by the fire with me," said Montano, taking my hand.

"This place is even nicer than I remember."

"Cozy, right?" he said, patting the sofa when I stopped to look at a photo on the mantel. "Don't tell me. That's Jimmy?"

I set the frame back where it had been and sat beside him.

"You should see my brother now," said Ranger, handing me the adult hot chocolate.

"Yeah? Got a dad bod?" asked Montano.

"Not exactly."

Ranger pulled out his phone, scrolled through his photos, and held it out for us to see. "That was taken this summer."

"Wow," I mumbled, marveling at how Jimmy Messick looked even better now than he did when we were teenagers.

"But he's married, right?" Montano chimed in.

Ranger shook his head and laughed. "He might be, but I'm not."

The man seated beside me made a growly noise in his throat.

"When did people start calling you Ranger?" I asked.

He sat in one of the chairs that flanked the sofa. "My first year of college."

"Where did you go?"

"I ended up at Syracuse, but I started out at the Ranger School in Wanakena."

"What made you change to Syracuse?"

He laughed. "Honestly, I was bored out of my mind."

"What did you study instead?"

I caught a look that passed between him and Montano, who nodded.

"I graduated with a degree from 'Cuse's Institute for Security Policy and Law Program. My emphasis was on Middle Eastern studies." He cleared his throat. "Enough about me. I was trying to remember the last time you were at the lake. I wasn't here much during high school since I was always in sports."

"Thirteen years, at least. Maybe even fourteen."

"You're my age, right? Two years younger than Jimmy?"

"That's right."

"When's the last time you checked in with the office?" Montano asked Ranger.

Ranger looked at him wide-eyed and up at the clock on the mantle. "It's nine o'clock."

"On the West Coast, it's only six."

I put my hand on Montano's arm.

"It's okay," said Ranger, noticing. "I was about to call it a night anyway."

We sat and stared at the fire for a few minutes without speaking. I was at a loss as to what to say, and he seemed just as bad.

"I'm sorry," he finally said. "I've never been a jealous person. And before you say I don't have any right to be, I know that. I can't explain it."

"Maybe it's just that you're used to getting all the attention."

He turned his body so he was facing me. "What makes you say that?"

"It was obvious your family dotes on you."

"That's just because they never see me."

"You're also charming and funny."

"I am?"

I slugged his arm. "You know you are."

"What about handsome? Am I that too?"

I rolled my eyes. "I've created a monster. Yes, Montano, you're very handsome. Another thing you know."

"Not as handsome as Jimmy, though."

"More handsome."

"Get out, sis. I saw you drooling over his photo on Ranger's phone."

"I wasn't drooling. I was just surprised. He doesn't look much different than he did all those years ago."

"You probably don't either."

"Oh, no. I do. At least, I hope so. I wasn't a very attractive teenager."

"Somehow, I doubt that."

"I'd show you a photo, but I've destroyed them all."

The playful look on Montano's face turned serious. "You're beautiful."

"Thank you," I whispered. "I know it's hard…"

He wriggled his eyebrows. "Oh, yeah? You noticed?"

I slugged him again and tried not to look at his crotch. I failed. But at least I tried not to. "What I meant was, I know it's difficult for you since I look so much like my sister."

"You don't look anything like her."

"Then, she must've really changed in the years since I last saw her."

Montano reached out and touched my cheek with his fingertip. "If the two of you were in a photograph, then yes, you'd look alike. But in person, flesh and blood, if she were here, I'd know in an instant who you were."

I couldn't stop myself from asking. "How? There were times I swear my parents weren't sure."

"So many things."

I rested my head against the back of the sofa.

"You don't believe me."

"It isn't that—"

"When we sat beside each other at Thanksgiving dinner and I looked into your eyes, I saw you, not Sofia. Every smile, I see you, not your sister. Your laughter, your mannerisms, your playfulness. I see you, not her."

"Are we really so different?"

13

Onyx

I put my finger on Blanca's chin and turned her head so she faced me. "Night and day. The desert and the ocean." An angel and a demon, I thought but didn't say.

"Most people thought we were the same. It's another reason I left. We couldn't find common ground, and it broke my heart."

Tears brimmed Blanca's eyes. I wanted to tell her she was better off without her sister in her life. She was better off not knowing who her sister had turned into before she died. But to do that, I had to admit I knew more than anyone else about the plane crash that took Sofia's life. The one Blanca knew next to nothing about except that her twin had died when it crashed.

"Maybe whatever it is you're meant to find will bring you some comfort."

"I don't know. To be honest, I'm not sure I even want to look."

"What do you mean?"

"I'm in over my head, Montano. I thought I could come here and reconnect with Sofia in a way I wasn't able to in the last few years of her life, but I can't. It's ridiculous to even try. The smartest thing for me to do is to hire an agent to sell the camp, and go home."

"By home, do you mean back to Italy?"

Blanca nodded. "It's been my home for a long time now."

"How about another hot chocolate?"

Her brow furrowed at my abrupt change in subject. "Sure, what the heck."

"That's the spirit," I teased.

When I came back from the kitchen, Blanca's eyes were closed. They opened when I sat beside her.

"I think you should stay," I blurted. "Get closure at the very least."

"Yeah?"

"Absolutely."

"What about you? How long will you be hanging out here at the lake?"

"As long as you are."

She sat up. "Why?"

I tucked a stray strand of hair behind her ear. "Because I want to."

"Don't you have to get back to work?"

"Most of what I do is remote anyway."

"How did you and my sister meet?"

"We were contracted as pilots to fly private aircraft."

"Oh. You're a pilot too?"

"Was."

"Why aren't you anymore?"

What I was about to tell her was mostly true. "When I started out, I flew F/A-18 Hornets. There's nothing like the thrill of piloting a fighter jet. Passenger jets, not so much. It kind of feels like driving a bus."

"I don't know much about my sister's career. When I left, she was talking about joining the Air Force."

"She flew F-15C Eagles."

"What's the difference between the two aircraft?"

"The F/A-18 was far superior." I laughed and so did she. "Seriously, though, there isn't much difference. The Hornet is newer. They're about the same size, but the F/A-18's wingspan is wider."

"You're competitive."

"I've been called that before."

"Sofia was competitive too. Far more than I ever was."

"You have no reason to be."

She nodded slowly, and the smile left her face.

"What I mean by that is, you excel without even trying."

The smile was back, along with a laugh. "Nice save, *bro*."

I laughed again too. "I'm serious. You're effortless. Everything you do comes naturally, and those around you marvel."

Her laughter turned into giggles. "You're so full of shit. You can stop blowing smoke up my skirt now."

I leaned forward so my mouth was near her ear. "It's true. You have no idea how amazing you are."

"You don't even know me," she whispered.

"Don't I?" I shouldn't kiss her. Everything in me knew that, but did that stop me? Hell no.

Blanca's tongue felt wet and hot as it twined with mine. I nipped her bottom lip, eliciting groans from her that reverberated deep in my chest. I pulled her onto my lap, holding her head with one hand so she didn't try to break the seal of our mouths. She did anyway.

"God, you're a good kisser," she mewled before angling her head and coming back for more.

"Good as the guys you write in your books?"

"Better. In fact, you're giving me lots of material."

I sneaked my hand under her sweater but rested it on her back. I was desperate to feel her bare skin, and as much as I wanted more, I knew I was already going too far just by kissing her.

I was breaking every rule, not just of my job, but that of my conscience too. I was seducing the twin sister of the woman who'd tried to kill me. The one I'd confessed my love to right before she pulled the trigger.

I knew that made me a sick fuck, but I couldn't stop myself. I wanted Blanca in a way I'd never wanted another woman—including and most especially, Sofia.

"We shouldn't be doing this," said Blanca, pulling away from me. Perhaps she sensed the struggle taking place in my head.

"My brain agrees; the rest of me doesn't."

She smiled. "That's honest, and I agree. Maybe we should call it a night."

"Good idea," I said, diving in for another scorching kiss.

I don't know how much time passed before we both pulled back, eyes glazed, lips swollen, bodies on fire.

"I should show you to your room."

She raised a brow.

"I promise I won't cross the threshold."

I stood, gathered her into my arms, and carried her up the stairs. As pledged, I stopped at the bedroom door and set Blanca on her feet.

"If you need anything, my room is the second door down the hall on the left. Second. Not first."

"I take it Ranger's is the first."

"You catch on quick."

"Montano—"

I stopped whatever she was going to say with another kiss. "Good night, angel."

She touched her lips, stepped inside the room, and closed the door behind her.

Angel. That's the way I saw her. The opposite of her twin, a demon incarnate.

Rather than going to my room, I went back downstairs, cleaned up the kitchen, and made sure the fire was almost out. When I turned to go back up, Ranger had come down.

"Everything okay?" he asked.

"About as far from it as it gets."

"We need to talk."

"Agreed. What I'm not certain we'll agree on is the topic."

"I have nothing to say about you and Blanca. You're both adults, and you need to handle this mission the way you see fit."

"Glad to hear it."

"Follow me."

Ranger led me out onto the enclosed porch and shut the door behind us.

"Damn cold out here, bro."

"This won't take long. What's the plan now that we've gotten her out of the camp, at least temporarily?"

"Her father told her it was imperative she find whatever Sofia left for her. His word choice confirms, at least to me, that it's some kind of evidence, most likely on a micro SD card."

"Which could be hidden just about anywhere."

"Sofia wanted it found, which means it can't be buried too deep. My guess is her father received a message about it after her death."

"It was an insurance policy."

"My thoughts exactly."

"Her plan was to kill you along with Tackle and Halo, land the plane, and complete her mission."

I nodded. Instead, Halo shot and killed Sofia first. At which point, we all should have died when the plane went down.

"I was serious earlier when I asked if you'd checked in with the office. Any word on Hatchet's whereabouts?"

"Hasn't moved."

"Has Wasp laid eyes on him?"

"Affirmative."

"As I said before, that means whoever sent him is arranging for a replacement."

"Do you want Wasp to stay on him?" Ranger asked.

"For now."

"Copy that."

"Have Diesel come in undercover tomorrow to deal with her power outage—which will stay out as long as we need it to."

"Roger that."

Given most of the camps sat empty at this time of the year, it wasn't like Blanca would get suspicious about hers being the only one without power.

Ranger put his hand on the door. "There's something I want to say before we go inside."

"What happened to you having nothing to say, bro?"

"I changed my mind."

"Change it back."

"Hear me out."

I nodded.

"I was trying to remember the last time Blanca was at the lake, because there was an incident with Sofia and my brother."

"What kind of incident?"

"Sofia made a play for him. I think at first she wanted him to think she was Blanca. When he called her out on it, she said it was a joke, but Jimmy was pissed."

"Did he tell Blanca?"

"I don't think so. I'm not sure he ever heard from her again."

"That it?" I asked since he still had a grip on the door and didn't appear to be going inside.

"I should've said something."

"I see." I motioned to two chairs. "Have a seat."

Before he sat down, he turned on the portable propane heater and cracked a window.

"Let it go, man. Someone making a play for their sister's boyfriend would never constitute a warning when we're vetting an agent, Ranger."

"I had a bad feeling about her. I should've spoken up."

"So did Dutch and he did speak up. I shot him down." I sat back in the chair, looked up at the ceiling, and back at him. "You wanna know how many times I ignored my instincts when it came to Sofia Descanso? Enough that Doc and Merrigan should fire me rather than have me head up a new K19 unit."

"Blanca is different."

"You sure about that? Cuz right now, I'm not certain my gut is trustworthy."

"You know she is. I do too."

"I hope to hell we're both right about her, bro. If not, and I manage to live through it, I'll be heading to somewhere in the Keys and run a fishing-boat business."

"That sounds pretty damn good either way."

The next morning, Diesel Jacks showed up after Ranger placed a call to the "electric company" on Blanca's behalf.

"It isn't just your place. We've got broken poles and primary wires down. You could be out for days."

"Days? As in, how many?"

"Hard to say. We've got lines down all over from this storm. Could be several."

"Great," she said after he left. "I guess I might as well head home."

"Nah. I have a better idea."

"What's that?"

"Why don't you show me around the Adirondacks instead?"

"I didn't spend any time here in the winter. Which, I suppose is obvious, given I didn't know the camp wasn't winterized."

"So, we play tourists together."

"What about Ranger?"

"He has work to do."

"Don't you?"

I put my arm around her shoulders. "I'm the boss, remember?" I turned her around. "First stop once we dig out of here is to get you some proper boots. While we're waiting, let's map out a plan."

14

Blanca

It took two days before the plow came to dig us out. During that time, we researched what there was to do in the area during the winter. The list was a lot longer than I thought it would be.

"The winter Olympics were in Lake Placid several years ago," Ranger reminded us. "Plus, Lake George is close by, as is Saratoga Springs."

"I remember going to horse races there."

"This afternoon, we can head out on the snowmobiles if you're up for it," he added, looking from me to Montano.

"Sounds good to me. We gotta get Blanca better boots, though."

Ranger hit the side of his own head. "I don't know why I didn't think of this sooner. My mom has all kinds of stuff she keeps here. It might be a little big on you, though. Come with me, and you can try some of it on."

"If you don't think she'd mind…"

"Of course she wouldn't. It's upstairs in the back bedroom closet."

When Ranger took a step in that direction, Montano grabbed his shoulder. "I'll take it from here, son."

"But—"

"Back bedroom closet, right?"

"Right," Ranger grumbled.

"I doubt he planned to stay in the room while I tried clothes on," I said, smacking Montano's arm.

"Not about to risk it."

"You're being a dork."

"What did you just call me? A dork? You're in big trouble now, sis."

I ran toward the stairs, giggling all the way, but didn't make it to the first step before he swept me up and tossed me over his shoulder. "Ouch!" I shrieked when he smacked my bottom playfully.

He carried me all the way upstairs and down the hallway as I tried to wriggle my way free. When we got to the bedroom, he set me down on my feet and opened the door.

"Go ahead. I'll be out here if you need my help with zippers or anything."

I play-swooned and put my hand on his chest. "So gallant. My protector and my savior."

Montano put his hand on top of mine and looked into my eyes. "I'll always protect you, angel. That's one thing you can count on." He let go and took a step back. "Get going before I change my mind and follow you into that room."

Everything I tried on fit me almost perfectly, even Ranger's mother's boots. It might have worried me since he thought his mom's clothes would be too big on me. However, I remembered her as always being petite.

"Whatcha got?" Montano asked when I came out of the room carrying two pairs of pants, two sweaters, and a pair of boots. "Doesn't look like much."

"If I need more, I know where to find it."

"What about a jacket?"

"I have mine."

"Which looks like a decent enough raincoat, but not something you can wear on the back of a snowmobile."

I rolled my eyes and shoved the clothes in my arms into his. "Fine. I'll grab a jacket."

"Look for snow pants too, sis," he shouted after me when I shut the door in his face.

An hour later, I was grateful for Montano's insistence that I borrow a warmer jacket, since even with it on, I was freezing.

"Let's stop in at the Canada Lake store and grab some sandwiches," suggested Ranger when we came off one trail that ended near the road.

Admittedly, I was starving, and as soon as he mentioned their sandwiches, I remembered how good they were. "Do they still have the Canada Laker?" I asked.

"The one with roast beef, cream cheese, and peperoncini?" Ranger asked. "Sure do. It's my favorite."

We ended up getting two Canada Lakers, a Wester—which had Italian cold cuts, provolone cheese, and oil and vinegar—along with the Caroga special, which was a turkey sandwich with cranberry sauce and stuffing.

Once we were back at Ranger's camp, we cut them into several pieces and shared them all. It was something I remembered my mom doing when we used to order out from them.

"I can't believe how much I've forgotten about being here," I said between bites. "Or how many of my memories are tied to food."

"Smells, too," said Montano. "I always hated being in the winery because I thought it stunk. When we were there at Thanksgiving, I felt more nostalgic when I walked in than nauseated."

"Nice one," muttered Ranger.

"Don't talk with your mouth full, son."

After we finished nearly every crumb, I could barely keep my eyes open. "I think I'll lie down for a while."

"I need to head into town to pick up a few things and arrange for another propane delivery. Onyx, you can come along or stay here, whichever you prefer."

"Maybe I'll lie down too," he answered, winking at me.

"You still awake?" I heard him say a few minutes later through my closed door.

"I am."

"Can I come in?"

"Of course."

"I brought an extra blanket in case you needed one, but your room is a lot warmer than mine is."

I smiled. "Thanks, but yeah, I'm good."

"I guess I'll just take this back to my cold room, then."

I smirked and patted the bed. Montano grinned and stretched out next to me. "If it's so cold in there, how come you haven't switched rooms?"

He spread the blanket over the two of us. "It isn't *that* cold, but it is definitely lonely."

I must've drifted off within seconds. When I woke, it was dark, but there was enough moonlight so I could see Montano was awake and staring at me.

"How long did I sleep?"

"Just a couple of hours."

"And how long have you been awake?"

"A few minutes."

"Is everything okay?"

"There's something you need to know."

I propped myself up on my elbows. "Go ahead."

"Even if your sister hadn't died in the plane crash, she and I wouldn't still be together."

"Why are you telling me this?"

"I like spending time with you, Blanca."

"As long as we're being forthcoming, I'll admit I like spending time with you too. However, I can't help but feel guilty about it."

He rested his head on the pillow and looked up at the ceiling. "I wish I'd met you first," he whispered. "Only so you didn't feel guilty."

"Me too."

When his phone buzzed, he sat up and looked at the screen. "Ranger wants to know if we're hungry again yet."

"Honestly, I'm starving. I know it hasn't been that long since we ate."

"Hey, I just realized something."

"What's that?"

"It's Friday."

"Yeah? Think anyone is serving fish fry?"

He held up his phone so I could see Ranger's text.

The Outlet is open and has real German potato salad, it read.

"You in?" he asked.

"Way ahead of you," I said behind me as I ran down the stairs to grab my boots and jacket.

I remembered the place as soon as we pulled up in front. "Norma and Eddie used to own the Outlet," I blurted, not really knowing where it came from.

"Who are Norma and Eddie?" asked Montano.

"No idea, other than that they owned it."

"Before my time," said Ranger, holding the door open for us.

"Can we sit at the bar?" I asked. For some reason, I remembered doing that too. "Genny Cream Ale for me," I said when the bartender asked what she could get me.

"You in?" Ranger asked.

"Make that three," Montano told her.

There were quite a few people in the place, considering the weather was so cold and crappy. Maybe that was why.

"Free drinks on me for whoever has lived around here the longest," Montano shouted out.

"Old Al has us beat," a woman said, pointing to a man and a woman who were in the midst of a conversation and appeared not to have heard the free drink offer.

"Yeah? How long has he been around here?"

"Hey, Al, how the hell old are ya?" one of the men hollered.

"Seventy-seven last Tuesday," he hollered back. "Who wants to know?"

"That feller over there is offering a free drink to whoever's lived here the longest."

"I know how old you are," said Montano. "But how long you been around here?"

"Born and raised here, son," Al answered.

"You know Norma and Eddie?"

"Sure do. So does she!" He pointed to the bartender.

"You do?" I asked.

"They were my parents."

"Is your name Veronica?"

"Nobody's called me anything but Ronnie for thirty years, but yeah, that's my name."

"You probably don't remember me—"

"Of course I do. You're Blanca Descanso. If that's still your name. One of these guys your husband?" She walked closer. "Wait a minute. You're Owen Messick. You didn't steal Blanca from your brother Jimmy, did you?"

Ranger laughed and shook his head. "No, ma'am."

"Who are you?" she asked Montano.

"Most people call me Onyx."

"Well, now I know you're married. Onyx and Blanca? That's sure as shit fitting."

"No, ma'am, we're not married," he told her.

She poured three beers and brought them over to us.

"Your sister around?" Ronnie leaned in and asked.

"No—"

"Gotta tell ya, I was never a fan of that one," she said before I could tell her my twin was dead. "I know she's your sister and all—"

"She passed away a year ago."

"Leave it to me to put my foot in it. I'm sorry, Blanca."

"Thanks."

"You okay?" Montano asked when she walked away.

I nodded, and he put his arm around my shoulders and leaned closer. "It's Friday night, and you know what that means—fishy fry," he whispered. "And what goes with fish fry? Genny Cream and a shot of Irish."

I nudged him and smiled. "Are you trying to get me drunk, bro?"

"You kiss me when you're drunk."

"You've got that backwards. You kiss me when you're drunk."

The man people called Al walked over to the juke-box, put some money in, and a few seconds later, music began to play.

"My dad and I used to dance to this," I murmured, singing along to Louis Armstrong's version of "Mack the Knife."

"Come on, then, sis. Dance with me." He held out his hand, I took it, and he spun me around the floor until I was breathless.

"You're a good dancer," I said when the song ended.

"Good dancer, good kisser…hmm. Wonder what else I might be good at?"

"Flirting. You're a pro at that."

When "I've Got You Under My Skin" began to play, Montano pulled me into his arms, and I remembered thinking the very thing about him that day on the Circle Line cruise.

"I'd sacrifice anything, come what may, for the sake of having you near. In spite of a warning voice that comes in the night and repeats, repeats in my ear," he sang, looking into my eyes. "I've got you under my skin."

When I tried to take a step back, he tightened his hold around my waist.

"I kiss you when I'm not drunk too, Blanca. What about you? Will you kiss me?"

Before I had a chance to respond, his lips were on mine. Unlike the impassioned kisses we shared before, this was more of a caress. It was unhurried, soft, two hungry mouths, wet and hot. No tongue, just lips.

When the song ended and Montano cupped my cheek and looked into my eyes, I was dizzy, stunned, my world rocked so hard I had to hold onto him for fear of my knees giving out.

"I've got you, deep in the heart of me. So deep in my heart that you're really a part of me."

"I've got you under my skin," I sang the words with him as we returned to the bar where Ranger sat, studying something on his phone.

"Everything okay, son?" Montano asked him.

"Uh, yeah. I, um, went ahead and ordered for us. Hope that's okay."

Ranger's eyes darted between Montano's and mine.

"If you gentlemen will excuse me," I said, pointing in the direction of the restrooms. As I went in, a very beautiful woman, one I hadn't noticed at the bar, came out of one of the stalls.

"Hi," I said when our eyes met.

"Hello," she responded in a British accent.

I went into the other stall and listened while she washed her hands and dried them, humming the song Montano and I had been dancing to.

There was something about the encounter that left me feeling unsettled. That, coupled with Ranger's strange behavior when we came back from dancing, pushed me over the edge into anxious.

15

Onyx

"Do you recognize him?" I asked Ranger when he handed me his phone. The image Diesel sent over was grainy and pixelated.

"I don't. I suggested he send it to Razor."

"Good thinking."

"He was scoping out our camp, not hers."

"Copy that."

"Diesel said he didn't even look in her windows."

I nodded, mulling over what Ranger had just said.

"Do you think you should relocate?"

I shook my head. "We've got plenty of backup. Let's see if he reappears later." I looked toward the restrooms in time to see Swan come out. We made eye contact before she went to the table she shared with Trap.

"What's he doing up here?" I asked Ranger.

"Hell if I know."

"Fucking McTiernan," I muttered under my breath.

Blanca had her arms wrapped around her waist when she came out a couple of minutes later. As she passed by, she glanced at Swan and then looked up at me.

"Everything okay?" I asked.

She shrugged. "I'm feeling out of sorts. Tired more than anything."

"We can get our fish fry to go if you want."

"Thanks, but believe me when I say it doesn't travel well."

I laughed, and she smiled, warming me all over. Damn, I liked this woman. Just like the song said, she was all the way under my skin. It was my thoughts of her body being under mine that jarred me back to reality.

While I'd crossed the line by kissing her, Blanca and I having sex was completely out of the question. No way in hell I could go down that road and come back with a clear conscience.

We left the restaurant as soon as we finished eating. Blanca was quiet throughout dinner and on the way back to the camps. Every attempt I made to get her to laugh resulted in a half-hearted chuckle.

When she went straight upstairs after thanking both Ranger and me and saying good night, I followed.

"You wanna talk about it?" I asked before she reached her bedroom.

"What do you mean?"

"Something happened at the restaurant."

She walked through the doorway but left it open, so I followed. I stood in front of her when she stopped by the bed.

"Tell me what happened."

"Nothing 'happened.' It's just so strange that Ronnie would say she wasn't a fan of my sister. I mean, how well did she even know her?"

"Some people just rub others the wrong way. It isn't always something easily defined."

"Out of the two of us, I would think that would've been me more than her."

I sat down on the edge of the bed and pulled her down beside me. "What makes you say that?"

"I told you I was my mother's favorite and Sofia was my father's."

"Yeah?"

"I have more of my mother's Germanic personality traits."

"Not following."

"From my experience living in Italy, they consider Germans aloof, cold, even secretive. Not as emotionally open as those with Latin blood—like my father."

"Again, I think you've got it backwards. Maybe your father and sister were close because she was less like him than you were."

Blanca shrugged. "You said we were as different as night and day."

"To me, you are."

"What happened between the two of you?"

There were many things I could say that would be the truth. We didn't feel the same way about each other. We were incompatible—considering she'd tried to kill me, that was definitely true. However, I gave her the same answer I would have if she'd asked about any other relationship I'd been in. "That was between your sister and me. Given she isn't here to tell you her side of the story, I don't feel right telling mine."

She bumped me with her shoulder and smiled. "That's fair. Figures you would be."

"I'm not sure I want to know what you mean by that."

"You're a decent guy, Montano."

"Decent? Ouch."

"You know I mean that in the best possible way."

When she flopped back on the bed and stared up at the ceiling, I did too.

"I can't pretend to know what you're going through, Blanca. I can't imagine losing one of my siblings, especially one I haven't spoken to in years. Compounding that is that Sofia was your twin. The only unsolicited advice I can give you is to allow yourself the time to process through this." I turned my head and saw her eyes close and a tear run down her cheek. "Do what you came here to do. You wanted to take this time to reconnect with your sister. Maybe finding whatever she left for you, will help you do that."

At this particular moment, I meant the words I'd just spoken. More, I wished I could make whatever she found something solely for her. No hidden messages, no insurance policies guarding against whoever Sofia worked for.

"Good advice," she said, wiping at her tears.

"However, I don't think you'll be able to look for it tomorrow. Another snowstorm is due to hit."

"Great. That'll mean even longer before they restore power."

"I have an idea."

She turned on her side and propped her head on her hand. "What's that?"

While I'd told Ranger I didn't think we should relocate, talking to Blanca now, I changed my mind. "Why don't we get up early tomorrow and drive up to Lake Placid? We'll hang out there a couple of days, and maybe by then, the electricity will be back on and you can resume your search."

"Resume? I haven't even started yet."

"Okay, then, you begin when we get back. I'll even promise to stay out of your hair and give you the time and space you need."

"Are you making that offer for me or for you?"

I turned on my side like she had. "For you. Why do you ask?"

"I don't want you to do that."

"No? I'm growing on you, right?"

She laughed. "Yeah, you're growing on me."

I reached out and cupped her cheek. "You tell me what you need, and I'll do my best to make it happen."

Blanca leaned forward and brushed my lips with hers. As much as I wanted to kiss her properly, with both of us lying on the bed together, that would be far too risky.

"I'll let you get some sleep," I said, sitting up.

"Thanks for making me feel better."

"I hope I did."

"You always seem to."

"We'll leave in the morning so we get up there before the storm hits here. Sound good?"

"Sounds perfect."

"Good night, Blanca."

"Good night, Montano."

"What's going on?" Ranger asked when I came downstairs.

"We're leaving in the morning for Lake Placid."

"I'm glad you reconsidered. It will give us time to search the camp without worrying about either her or someone else discovering us. So, uh, what was wrong?"

"The bartender's comments about her sister got her down."

"I get that. I can badmouth Jimmy all I want, but when someone else does, it pisses me off."

"Do me a favor and find whatever the hell Sofia left behind before Blanca does. If it's what we think it is, try to find something else to put in its place. Something sentimental."

"Like what?"

"Shit, I don't know. Look while you're there. Better yet, have Swan look for something."

"Onyx…"

"You got somethin' to say, son, spit it out."

"Forget it." He shut off the lights in the kitchen. "I'm going up. Let me know when you're ready for me to relieve you."

"Roger that."

While Diesel, Swan, and now Trap, were ensconced in Blanca's family's camp and surveilling both structures' perimeters, Ranger and I were responsible for monitoring the interior of this camp.

"By the way, Cowboy arrived this morning. He can accompany you to Lake Placid. Diesel, Swan, and I will continue looking for whatever Sofia left."

"Don't forget Trap."

"Do you want him to go to Lake Placid with you?"

"Negative. Have Buster take over Hatchet's detail and get Wasp up here. *Tonight.* He can go with us."

"Roger that."

The farther we got on our three-hour drive from Canada Lake to Lake Placid, the better the weather became. By the time we arrived, the clouds had disappeared, leaving a deep-blue sky and lots of sunshine.

I'd made arrangements for an early check-in at the Adirondack Lodge where I'd booked a two-bedroom cabin. It sat right on the water and had a deck that stretched its entire length. The location offered us easy access to snowshoeing and cross-country skiing trails too.

"When I was growing up, Lake Placid seemed so far away. I can't believe it was this close and we never visited," said Blanca when I found her on the deck, looking out at the expanse of the lake.

"I lived thirty minutes from the beach and never went." I handed her a bottle of the beer we picked up on the way here.

Blanca sat in one of the Adirondack chairs, and I sat in another. "Why do you think that is?"

I took a swig of the beer I brought out for myself. "A lot of reasons. Us kids were expected to work in the vineyards. For me, I wanted out of there so bad, I spent all my free time studying."

"You could've studied at the beach."

"I take it nothing stopped you from seeking out new adventures."

"Not once I had a car. And enough money for a plane ticket."

"Speaking of money, do you need to be working?" I couldn't help but wonder if she was as obsessed with it as her sister had been. So far, I hadn't seen any indication she was.

"By working, do you mean writing?"

"Yeah, although I'm sure there's a lot more to it than that."

"Words on paper is definitely the most important part. Research is second to that. Once I'm done with a story and it moves into editing and stuff like that, I lose interest."

"Onto the next?"

"You'd laugh if I told you how many ideas for books I have sitting in an imaginary queue, waiting for me to get to them."

"How many?"

"More than thirty."

"How long will it take you to write that many books?"

"At this rate?"

I laughed. "Normally."

She shrugged. "Between four and five years."

I gasped. "For thirty books?"

"Give or take. Does that seem like a lot or a little?"

"Uh, I would've guessed at least a year each. Are all authors that prolific?"

"Some write more. Some less. Everyone writes at their own pace. That varies, of course, by circumstance. Writer's block is a real thing."

"Are you writing anything now?"

Blanca leaned against the chair, closed her eyes, and breathed deeply. "I was. I don't know if I'll finish it."

"Why?"

"It isn't what I usually write."

A bad feeling settled in my chest. "You're writing your sister's story, aren't you?"

"Trying. Although, I don't have a helluva lot to work with. I know next to nothing about her life in the last eleven years. Even less about how she died. I mean, I can't understand why there are no details available about the plane crash. Isn't there a black box or something?"

"It can take months before definitive conclusions about the cause of a crash can be reached."

Blanca opened her mouth, closed it, and opened it again before getting up, going inside, and closing the door behind her.

I got up and followed. "Did I say something wrong?"

She finished her beer and pulled another out of the refrigerator. "You sounded exactly like the people I've already spoken to."

"It's a simple fact, sis."

She set her beer on the counter hard enough that some spilled from the top. "Don't call me that."

I stared into Blanca's eyes, waiting for her to say something more. When she didn't, I took a deep breath. "I'm sorry. Most of the time, I don't realize I'm doing it. I'll be careful not to again."

"Why are you here?"

"What do you mean?"

"First, you showed up in Manhattan, saying you were there on business. That turned into taking time off and going to the lake, but you don't seem to be in any hurry to leave. Neither does Ranger."

I walked around the island that separated us and took her hands in mine. "You're right. There are things I need to tell you. Some of it might not make a lot of sense."

Blanca pulled her hands away and ran one through her hair. "Oh my God."

I took a step closer and smiled. "I haven't said anything yet."

"Are you going to tell me something—anything—about my sister?"

"Yes."

She put a hand on her hip. "Go ahead."

"Let's have a seat."

Instead of sitting on the sofa, Blanca chose a chair. I pulled up an ottoman, sat in front of her, and put my hands on the chair's arms.

"I'm going to start out with questions, but I promise I'll also give you answers."

She nodded.

"Do you know anything at all about Sofia's career in the Air Force or what she did after she separated from the service?"

"I know she flew F-15C Eagles." She smiled and so did I. "What does separated from the service mean?"

"It's a new way of saying someone was discharged."

"Oh. You also said the two of you met when you were both contracted to fly private planes."

"That's right. Who have you spoken with about the crash?"

"I can't recall his name. I have it written down, though."

"Do you know what agency he was with?"

"He didn't say."

"The company that contracted Sofia and me to fly for them is owned by former military, some former intelligence."

"Do you still work for them?"

"I do. Although not in the same capacity."

Her hands gripped the arms of the chair, but not close enough to touch mine. "Am I in danger?"

"What makes you ask that question now?"

"Someone came looking for me in Paso Robles, even though no one knew I was there. Then, like I said, you showed up in Manhattan." Her breathing slowed, and her eyes bored into mine. "Am I in danger from you?"

I put my hands on hers. "Blanca, ask yourself that question. Do you believe I'd harm you?"

"My gut says no, but that doesn't mean my gut is right."

God, if she only knew what she was saying. "No, you are not. I promised to protect you. Do you remember?"

"Yes." She bit her bottom lip. "Am I in danger because I'm looking for information about the crash?"

"There are a lot of unanswered questions about it as well as what your sister might have been working on when it happened. The people I work for are searching for those answers."

"But they aren't the only ones."

"That's right."

"The guy on the boat and the guy on the bridge—were they the same person?"

It figured that someone who wrote books would possess the kind of imagination that would immediately fill in blanks, piece stories together in the way Blanca was.

"I believe so."

"Was I in danger from him?"

"What did he say to you, Blanca?"

"Nothing really. He was trying to make conversation. He asked if I was from New York and if I'd ever been to Yankee Stadium."

"Is there anything else he asked that you can recall?"

"Right after that, he looked distracted. He walked away and down the aft stairs without saying another word. Then, I thought I saw him on the bridge. He saw you and got off the boat, didn't he?"

"He saw more than just me."

"Right. You and Ranger. You're both so chummy with me, but really, you're watching me." Blanca tried to push my arms out of her way and stand, but I wouldn't budge.

"We're protecting you."

"There's more to it, though, isn't there? You're the ones looking for information on behalf of the people you work for." She put her hand in front of her mouth and gasped. "It's what Sofia left for me, isn't it? That's why my father said it's imperative I find it."

"It's possible, yes." I leaned in closer. "Blanca, look at me."

She shook her head and kept her gaze focused on the wall.

"Please, look at me."

"I don't want to," she said, but she slowly turned her head.

"From the moment I met you, I felt a connection. I know you did too. It's difficult for both of us because I was with your sister. However, everything I've said about how different I think you are from her, all the fun we've had together, that is all separate from what you're searching for."

"I don't know how to believe you."

I slid off the ottoman and knelt in front of her. "Do you think it's possible to fake how this makes both of us feel?" I grasped the back of her neck and brought my lips to hers. Like every other time I kissed her, Blanca's mouth opened to mine. Our tongues twined and our teeth clashed as the passion between us intensified.

I moved my hands to her waist and pulled her close to me so I was between her legs. "I want you, Blanca, even though I know neither of us is ready to take that step. I can't pretend otherwise. I'd give anything to have met Ranger all those years ago, been invited to his camp, and swept you off your feet before Jimmy had the chance to."

16

Blanca

I stared into Montano's eyes, looking for any sign of a lie. Any flinch. Any eye movement I could construe as evidence that he wasn't being honest with me. There was nothing. Either this man was a master at playing women like they were his own personal fiddle or he was telling me the truth.

There were enough times when we'd been close that I knew he was as turned on as I was. Only briefly had I wondered if his attraction to me was a manifestation of my sister. I immediately deemed the idea ludicrous, and then more so when the mere mention of her appeared to darken his mood.

Something had obviously happened between them that left Montano bitter toward Sofia.

When I set out to learn more about my sister, my expectation had been that I would discover she was how I'd always imagined her to be—popular, sought after, the life of the party, everyone's best friend. I'd heard none of that, from anyone. Even the bartender of a restaurant we'd frequented as teenagers.

Montano said some people just rubbed others the wrong way, yet the reactions I'd witnessed seemed more intense than superficial dislike.

If I thought about my own feelings alongside the feelings of others who'd shared theirs, I couldn't lie to myself and say I didn't feel the same way.

The bottom line was, I hadn't liked my sister since we were little girls. It was only the pressure I felt to be like "other twins" that kept me from admitting it out loud. Weren't we supposed to be closer to one another than anyone in the world? I'd never felt that way about her. In fact, there were times I wondered if she wished I hadn't been born.

I knew other siblings fought, said hateful things, especially with two teenage girls involved. But it had always felt worse than that. It was one of the reasons I'd left. It wasn't just that I no longer believed I fit in with her and my father; it was I had to get away from her.

"Blanca?" said Montano when I took a deep breath and let it out slowly. "What's going on?"

"I just realized something."

"Tell me."

"I left because I didn't want to be like her."

"Sofia?"

"Yes. I hated the way she'd make everyone think she didn't have a care in the world. She was the fun one, the passionate one, the one I thought everyone wanted to be around. But at home, she was someone else entirely." I took another deep breath, giving myself time to be sure I really wanted to say the words I was about to.

"We don't have to talk about this anymore tonight."

"No. I want to. Even though what I'm about to say may change your mind about me."

"I doubt that, but go ahead."

"Remember I told you I knew when she died? I felt it."

"Yes."

"It was relief, Montano. I felt a great weight lift from my shoulders, and I just *knew* she was gone. I know I'm being dramatic. I'm practically demonizing her, and that isn't my intention. She was my sister, and I loved her. There were just too many instances when I didn't like her."

He eased away and sat back on the ottoman. "Hard on my knees," he explained, rubbing them.

"Would it help if we sat on the sofa?"

"Not sure how much it would help my knees, but my heart would really like it."

I rolled my eyes but smiled. "You're such a flirt." I stood and held my hand out to him. "Come on, *old man*. Let's get you comfortable."

Montano took his time getting up, but once he was, fast as lightning, he picked me up and tossed me over his shoulder like he had a couple of nights ago. Then he'd carried me upstairs.

"Now that you've got me here, what will you do with me?" I couldn't resist teasing him.

"I'm thinking about tossing your *young* perky ass in a pile of snow."

"What's stopping you?"

He shook his head and laughed. "I promised to protect you. What if you get pneumonia or something? I wouldn't exactly be living up to my word."

"Tell you what, why don't you toss me on my bed instead?"

He moved closer to the sofa and deposited me there, much to my chagrin. That he sat down and put his arm around my shoulders didn't do much to alleviate my embarrassment. "If I thought you were really ready to share a bed with me, that's where we'd be."

"We can lie on a bed and not have sex. We did the other night."

"You must've missed the part when I bolted upright and rushed out of there."

"Oh. God, now I really feel like a dork."

"No, it wasn't you, Blanca. It was me. I was so close to putting my hand under your shirt, teasing the nipples that were straining so hard to get my attention, tasting more than your lips, touching more than your cheeks, your neck, your hands."

"Why didn't you?" I whispered.

"We aren't ready for that, and you know it."

I wanted to tell him he was wrong, but he wasn't. Having sex with Montano now would be a huge mistake. We hardly knew each other. On top of that, any insecurities lingering in my head that he was only attracted to me because I was a replacement for my sister would grow until I had no choice but to get away from him. Fair or not, logical or not, I knew that's how I'd react. He was absolutely right. Neither of us was ready for sex.

I rested my head on his chest and put my arm around his waist. "I feel like I told you a lot more about my sister than you told me."

"We may be done for now, but we aren't done talking. If you have questions, I'll answer them the best I can."

"I'm too emotionally drained to talk more tonight."

"Are you too tired for food?"

He sounded so much like a little boy, I laughed. "I'm never too tired to eat, Montano. Haven't you figured that out yet?"

"Do you like to cook?"

"Um…like to cook? I'm not even sure what that means."

"You know, barefoot, in the kitchen, heavenly scents wafting from whatever you're stirring on the stove."

"Uh, no. That wouldn't be me. I'm more of a sneak-into-the-kitchen-and-steal-a-taste-of-what-someone-else-is-cooking kind of girl. What about you? Do you like to cook?"

"I'm not sure I could say I like it, either. Although, I don't think I'm as bad as you are."

"Bad? Not liking to cook makes me *bad*? I think it just makes me lazy."

"I may have seen a room service menu in the kitchen." He started to get up, but I pushed him back into the cushions.

"I'll get it," I said, waiting until I was far enough away that he couldn't grab me before adding, "Don't want you to hurt your knees."

I found the menu he'd referred to, sitting on the counter. The kinds of things on it were why I didn't cook. I mean, why cook when I could order a bone-in Kansas City dry-aged rib eye with grilled lobster tail, scallops, and shrimp? Or English pea soup, also served with grilled lobster, but with the addition of trout caviar and mint-lemon créme fraiche.

While I should've stopped there, I didn't. I also chose candied salmon with maple-glazed slab bacon and cheddar grits plus an Adirondack charcuterie board that came with local cheeses, cured meats, paté, pickled vegetables, olives, crab-apple mustard, and fresh-baked bread.

"What sounds good?" Montano asked from the other room.

"Um, kind of a lot. I went ahead and ordered a few things. I hope that's okay," I answered, returning to the sofa and sitting beside him.

"You didn't steer me wrong with the fish fry. I trust your taste." He rubbed both his ears. "I didn't even hear you. Must be the altitude change."

"Actually, they had a tablet on the counter, so I just ordered online."

"I only skimmed the menu. You didn't happen to order oysters, did you?"

I bit my lower lip. "I didn't, but I can."

"Will you eat some?"

"Yes. I love oysters," I answered, walking to the kitchen to place the additional order.

"And maybe a bottle of wine?"

"You're taking this 'don't hurt your knees' thing very seriously," I shouted back at him from the kitchen, where I was studying the wine list.

"What did you say?" I jumped when I felt Montano brush against me.

"You startled me."

"And you were making fun of me."

"Yeah? What are you going to do about it?"

"I don't know, but maybe this will give me some ideas." He held up a tablet of his own, and on it was the cover of one of my books.

"How did you find that?"

"It wasn't difficult." He pointed first to the letter B. "For Blanca." Then the letter D. "For Dawn, your middle name, and finally, Pfeiffer, your mother's maiden name."

"I'm not sure which disturbs me the most. You searching for one of my books or that you know my middle name." He set the tablet down without commenting on the title of the particular book he chose, *Temptress,* and I was relieved he didn't tease me about it.

I wasn't ashamed of the books I wrote; I'd just grown weary of people who believed they could say whatever they wanted about them and me, as if I weren't a living, breathing person with feelings.

"Neither should disturb you. I searched for your books because I'm looking forward to reading them. As for your middle name, I knew it began with D, but I guessed it was Dawn."

"Who guesses Dawn? Wouldn't Diana be more likely or Debbie?"

Montano scrunched his nose and laughed. "Debbie?"

"I shouldn't be surprised you knew my mother's maiden name. I'm sure Sofia told you."

"She didn't. I read it in a brief I was given a few days ago."

"A *brief*? About me?"

"That's right. It's also the real reason I knew your middle name." He cleared his throat. "What I'm about to tell you may or may not come as a surprise."

I pulled out a kitchen chair and sat. "You could've waited until I had at least one glass of wine."

"I figured the beer counted."

"Not as high a level of alcohol by volume. Enough about booze. What may or may not surprise me?"

"Until you showed up at my family's home for Thanksgiving, I was unaware you existed."

That didn't come as a surprise at all. My cheeks still burned in embarrassment, though. I could feel them. "I didn't show up for Thanksgiving. I didn't even remember the holiday."

Montano held out his hand and, when I took it, pulled me up from the chair, sat in my place, and positioned me on his lap. "There is a possibility your sister intentionally hid your existence to protect you."

"Right." I tried to get up, but he put his arm around my waist.

"I want you to think about what I just said."

"Okay."

"You asked if you were in danger, and I'm going to tell you straight that you are. There was video surveillance of the man who came to Los Caballeros looking for you."

"Someone you recognized?"

Montano nodded. "You would recognize him too."

His hold on me tightened as I processed what he'd just said. "Oh my God, it was the man from the boat."

"It was."

"Do you think he followed us here?" I felt sick to my stomach and regretted ordering all that food.

"I know he didn't."

"You have someone following him, don't you?"

"Yes. Someone has been following us as well."

"Good guy or bad guy?"

"Good ones, definitely. Bad ones, I hope not, but if any did, you're protected."

Everything that had happened since Montano approached me on the tour boat raced through my mind. "The driver in New York City. He works for you, doesn't he?"

"Yes. His name is Buster Franks."

"Who else?"

"The guy from the electric company."

I stared him down. "Seriously? You *pretended* I lost power? I could've frozen to death."

He ran a finger down my cheek. "How long after your power went out did I knock on your door?"

"I don't know. A few minutes."

"Not even two minutes. I told you I'd protect you, angel, and I meant it."

"Angel? Is that one of those things you do? You're calling me that instead of sis?"

Montano shook his head. "I'm calling you that because it's the way I see you."

"You're just saying that so I stop being mad about the electricity." There was a knock at the door, and I almost screamed.

"It's our dinner," Montano said as if he could see through the door, and he wasn't facing it.

"How can you be sure?"

"I got a text that Cowboy would be delivering it at six on the dot." He scooted me off his lap and stood.

"He can eat mine. I'm not hungry anymore."

"I don't believe that for a minute." He put his hand on the doorknob but didn't open it. "I'm going to invite him in so you know what he looks like. There's one other person who came with us on this trip. His name is Wasp. You can meet him in the morning."

Montano waved his hand at the man carrying the basket of food. "Come in, Cowboy. I want you to meet Blanca."

"There's more food to bring in."

"Is Wasp out there?"

The man he'd called Cowboy nodded.

"Good. Tell him to come in."

"Ma'am," he said, tipping his hat at me before he went out the door he'd come in.

"Is he for real?" I whispered.

"One hundred percent."

He came back inside, followed by another man; both were carrying baskets.

"I may have overdone the food order a little."

The man I hadn't met yet set his basket down and held out his hand. "I'm Jasper Theron, but most everyone calls me Wasp."

The cowboy was right behind him. "Garrison Cassidy. It's a pleasure to meet you."

"Blanca is aware of the danger we believe she may be in. She's also aware of Diesel's and Buster's involvement."

"Is there anyone else? Other than Ranger, I would assume."

"Two more. A woman who goes by Swan and one other man, Trap."

"The woman I saw at the restaurant. Was that her?"

"It was," answered Montano. "She was having dinner with Trap."

"She's very beautiful," I muttered under my breath.

I felt Montano behind me before I heard him. "She doesn't hold a candle to you, angel," he whispered in my ear before taking a step away. "Okay, gentlemen, if you have nothing to report, you can clear out so we can eat."

"Nice to meet you both," I said as they left.

"Where should we start?" he asked.

"Oysters?"

"I like the way you think."

"I'll open the wine."

"I like that even more."

17

Onyx

Blanca was as observant as she was smart. As soon as I told her everything I had, I decided she needed to know about the team on her detail and what they looked like—at least the two here with us. After we ate, I'd put their contact information into her phone as well.

"This is a ridiculous amount of food. I'm sorry."

"Sorry? Are you kidding? I'll eat whatever you don't and order dessert on top of it."

She laughed. "Consider this an official challenge. We have to set a time limit, though."

"I'm up for it. What are you thinking?"

"It's six fifteen now. Two hours?"

"No problem."

She smirked. "You're on."

"Is there some kind of wager involved?"

"Do you think there should be?"

Oh yeah, I did, but everything I could come up with involved Blanca being in various stages of undress.

"Your face is expressive."

I looked up from the oysters. "Is it?"

"Very."

"Are you saying you know what I'm thinking?"

"I'm saying that if you're thinking what I think you are, you shouldn't eat any more of those oysters."

I sat back in the chair. "This is just a trick to keep them all for yourself, isn't it?"

Blanca slowly shook her head. "Since I'm thinking the same thing you are, I shouldn't have any more either."

I laughed out loud, and so did she, and then we polished off the remaining so-called aphrodisiacs.

If we'd wagered, I would've lost because she was right; there was no way I could finish everything she'd ordered, even with Blanca eating her share of it.

"You bested me, woman."

She rubbed her belly. "I'm so full I have to go to sleep."

"Go ahead, I'll clean up."

"I can help."

"Nah, you ordered."

She smiled and shook her head. "Thanks for today," she said, leaning down and kissing my cheek. "Thank you for respecting me enough to tell me what's going on."

"You deserved to know. It's your life."

"Sleep well." Blanca waved behind her as she walked out of the kitchen.

I thanked her even though I had no intention of sleeping. Truth be told, I couldn't wait to get started on her book.

I put as much of the food away as I could, double-checked the doors and windows were secured everywhere but the room Blanca was in, and then remembered I hadn't put Wasp's or Cowboy's cell numbers in her phone like I meant to do.

"Knock, knock," I said, tapping lightly and hoping she wasn't asleep yet.

"Just a sec." It took her a minute to open the door, and then it was only a crack. "What's up?"

"There's something I need to do."

"Oh, uh, give me another minute, okay?"

I rested against the wall and tried my hardest not to allow my mind to imagine everything she might have been doing before I knocked. Instead, it raced with it. Had she gone into her bedroom intending to take care of any desires brought on by our conversation about the oysters? I knew as soon I was alone, that's what I'd be doing.

I groaned when all I could picture was Blanca under her bedsheets, one hand between her legs, the other playing with her nipples. I reached into my jeans to adjust myself at the same moment she reopened her door. My hand froze where it was, and time seemed to stand still as she looked from my eyes to my groin.

"Is there anything I can do to help?" The idea that she was teasing me was almost enough to make my problem go away, until my eyes met hers and I saw the heat in them. I slowly moved my hand.

"I, um, wanted to check and make sure your bedroom window was secured."

She took one step closer. "You could've asked me to do that myself."

"I also meant to give you contact info for Cowboy and Wasp."

"Why?"

"Just in case you needed to reach them for anything."

She took one more step. *"Anything?"*

I grabbed her shoulders and spun her around so her back was against the wall. "No. Not anything," I said, my lips close enough to hers to touch. "What were you doing in there?"

She raised her chin. "Book research."

"Jesus," I groaned before my mouth came crashing down on hers. I put my hands on her ass, digging my fingertips into her flesh, and lifted her. "Put your legs around me," I demanded, instinctively grinding myself against her heat. "I'll take care of anything you need, Blanca. Do you understand me?"

"Will you?" Her arms tightened around my neck, and I kissed her hard. My tongue delved in to slide against hers; my body pressed her against the wall. Lust warred against my conscience when she slid one hand under my shirt while the fingers of the other wove into my hair.

When she rolled her hips, I came as close as I had in over a year to having an orgasm brought on by another person. Unable to resist another second, I slid my hand inside the back of the sweatpants she must've pulled on in order to come out of the room to talk to me.

I moaned in frustration, knowing I had to stop, when my fingers brushed up against the soft lace of the panties that clung to the curves of her perfect ass. I broke our kiss with a nip at her bottom lip and lowered her legs to the ground.

Blanca's chest heaved, her eyes glazed over, and her lips were damp and swollen.

Before I changed my mind, I walked into her bedroom and checked the lock on the window. "I'll give you those numbers tomorrow, angel," I said when she met me at the door.

"Are you seriously about to say good night to me?"

Knowing that if I touched her again, I wouldn't be able to stop myself from fucking her senseless, I put my hands in my pockets. "Consider what just happened more book research."

Yeah, it was an asshole move, but it would have been far worse had I followed through and had sex with her.

An hour later, I woke to the sound of someone screaming. In horror, I grabbed my gun and tore out of the bedroom in the direction of the sound.

"Blanca? What happened?" I raced to put her behind me when I saw her pointing at the door.

"B-b-bear," she stammered.

I shut off the kitchen lights and stepped forward to look out one of the windows. Blanca had a firm grasp on my boxer briefs. "Put your arms around my waist instead, angel."

"Where are you going?"

"I want to see if he or she is still close by."

"What if it's still on the deck?"

"You're right. I should call for backup."

"Who are you going to call?"

"Wasp."

She nodded but didn't let go of my waist as I turned to go back into the bedroom.

"Where are you?" I asked when he answered.

"Watching a couple of rangers trying to get a mama bear safely away from your cabin."

"Any sign of cubs?"

"Negative, and before you ask, I figured you were both asleep when I didn't see any lights on, so I didn't alert you. I saw the bear heading onto the deck, but I didn't think it would be wise to take it on myself, so Cowboy called the local sheriff. The rangers arrived shortly after."

"Copy that. Send me an update when you have one." I hung up and turned in Blanca's arms. "I'm sure you heard all of that."

She nodded.

"What do you say we try to get some sleep?"

"There is no way I'll be able to sleep now."

"You know there are probably all kinds of critters roaming around outside at night, and you're never the wiser."

Her eyes were wide. "Was that supposed to make me feel *better*?"

I inched the two of us closer to the bed. "You can sleep in here tonight."

"Where will you be?"

"I don't think it would do much to alleviate your fears if I wasn't beside you, would it?"

"No."

I pulled back the sheets, waved her in, and she scooted over.

"Be right back." I pulled on a pair of sweats, went out to the kitchen, and checked the deck and what else I could see, but there was no sign of activity. Fine by me. I made a pit stop in the bathroom and hoped by the time I came out, Blanca would be asleep.

Wishful and foolish thinking since she was sitting up in bed, staring at the wall, when I lay beside her. "You okay?"

"Yeah. Just not sure I'll be able to sleep."

"What do you usually do when you can't?"

"Write."

"Go ahead. It won't bother me."

"You'll be able to sleep through me tapping away on my keyboard?"

"It'll probably soothe me."

"You're weird."

I opened one eye, and she winked.

"You could always read me a bedtime story first." I wiggled my eyebrows.

"And a dork."

I reached out, pinched her waist, and she giggled.

"I'll go get my laptop if you're sure I won't keep you awake."

"I'll get it. Just tell me where it is."

"On my bed. I'll probably need the charger that is connected to it too."

The laptop was open when I went into the room, but rather than look at the screen, I closed it. I'd probably never sleep if I read it and she was in the middle of writing a sex scene.

Just the thought that she might be brought my cock from half asleep to wide awake.

I handed her the computer, got on the bed with my back to her, and willed my mind to think about anything other than sex. I closed my eyes and thought about Blanca on the day we met.

It seemed that since I got over the initial shock of seeing her, every memory was a good one. She was beautiful, quick-witted, earnest, and even when she got mad at me, got over it quickly. Another trait her sister hadn't developed.

I opened one eye when I felt her leaning against my shoulder. Correction: all I could really feel were her breasts. "Yes?"

"You can't be asleep yet."

"I wasn't."

"Are you sure about this? I mean, I could go into the other room now. I'm over seeing the bear."

"I'm not. Me offering to let you sleep here was more for me than you."

"I don't believe you."

"First a weirdo, then a dork, and now a liar. You don't have a very high opinion of me, do you?"

"Actually, I can't think of anyone I have a higher opinion of than you."

"Ditto."

18

Blanca

Instead of going back to what I'd been writing, I opened a new document. I couldn't concentrate on anything other than the man beside me, so I decided to let him be my muse.

The thing I understood least about him was his reaction to happily-ever-after endings the day we ran through Central Park. From everything I'd seen, Montano was every woman's fantasy of the perfect man. He was extraordinarily good-looking, with a ripped body, and had a great sense of humor. He was smart, charming, flirtatious, and had not only promised to protect me, but he'd followed through when I went into the kitchen for a glass of water, saw a bear staring at me through the glass door, and screamed.

He'd gallantly offered to let me sleep with him, and while I would love to feel his naked body next to mine, the chivalrous way he put on sweatpants and lay on top of the covers made me swoon.

While all of that should be enough to make any woman throw herself at him, that he'd pushed me up against the wall, kissed me breathless, and in a growly voice, told me he'd be the one to take care of whatever I needed, made my panties melt.

So what was the deal with him not believing in the fairy-tale ending? It would be one thing if he was skeptical or questioning, but his reaction had been more than that. He could see the beginning and middle of the love story, but couldn't fathom the ending.

Was it my sister's doing that Montano no longer believed loved could last? Something told me there had been a time in his life when he had.

My hands gripped the steering wheel hard when I turned onto the road I hoped would lead me to the person who could give me answers about my sister—my dead twin sister.

Was it my best opening line ever? Definitely not. But like I'd told Montano earlier, the book I was writing presently wasn't the kind I normally wrote. This was a different book than the one I'd been talking about at the time, but as my fingers flew on the keyboard, I knew this was the one I had to write.

I stretched my arms over my head, opened my eyes, and looked around the sunlit room. It took me a minute to remember where I was.

The bed beside me was empty, but the smell of coffee brewing somewhere close wafted into the room. That wasn't all. Accompanying that heavenly scent was that of bacon frying.

I rolled out of bed and felt the cold cover of my laptop under my toes when I went to stand. Instead, I scooted down the bed, and put my feet on the equally chilly hardwood floor of the cabin.

Instead of putting on my sweatpants, I picked up a sweatshirt that, by its size, had to belong to Montano and pulled it over my head. As I'd expected, it was long enough that it covered my knees.

The only other thing I put on was a pair of warm, woolly socks before I sneaked out of the bedroom and across the hallway to the bathroom. I couldn't say for sure why I didn't want Montano to see me yet, other than I'd written a scene last night where the heroine surprises the hero by sneaking up behind him and wrapping her arms around his waist, and decided I wanted to act it out in real life.

Sadly for my original fantasy, he was facing my direction when I walked into the kitchen. However, his eyes trailing from my bed-ravaged hair down my body was a scene I'd happily write later.

"Good morning, angel," he said, motioning to the breakfast set out on the kitchen table.

I raised my eyebrows, surveying his bare chest and the way his sweats hung low on his hips that I found more mouthwatering than the food.

"You fried bacon topless. Brave man."

"It's character building. You should try it."

"Maybe tomorrow."

"We could have BLTs for lunch if you don't want to wait."

I gave him a half smile. "Did I smell coffee?"

He reached over to the counter and handed me a cup.

"Is this for me?"

He made like he was looking around me on both the left and the right. "Don't see anyone else here, angel."

I took a sip and walked over to the chair he'd pulled out for me. "Wow, this is good."

"How do you like your eggs?"

"It doesn't matter to me. Any way you like them."

I savored my coffee, sneaked a piece of bacon, and listened to Montano hum as he cooked the eggs. "I wonder what happened with the bear."

"They took her to wherever her cubs were. I guess she and they were tagged."

"It's a marvel, isn't it? That they can do that."

He didn't respond, and when I looked over my shoulder, I saw him studying his phone.

"Everything okay?"

He set it down on the counter, plated the eggs, and joined me at the table.

"Montano?"

"We weren't the only ones who had a visitor last night."

"No?"

"The crew at Canada Lake had one too. Someone different than the one we had the night before we left."

I felt my stomach drop. "The night before we left?"

"Sorry, angel. I guess I didn't tell you about that."

"What kind of visitor?"

"Someone we believe is working with Hatch."

"He gave me his real name?"

"Did he?"

"Richard Hatch."

"That's right. Although he's known more as Hatchet."

Now I felt sick to my stomach. I'd shifted to get up from the table when Montano put his hand on my shoulder.

"The more we talk about it, the less frightening it will be."

"I'm not so sure about that."

"The team protecting you is made up of some of the best men and women I've ever worked with. I hand-picked each of them. We aren't going to let anyone get to you."

"You said the visitor was someone working with Hatchet."

"A known associate, yes."

I held up my hand. "Please don't tell me his name until I've finished eating."

"Her name."

"Interesting."

"Makes sense for this type of job."

I'd ask him to elaborate, but I really didn't want to talk about it, no matter what he said about it being less frightening if we did. "Do we need to leave?"

"If you mean here, no. It isn't you they're after. It's what they believe Sofia left behind."

"Your people are looking for it, aren't they?"

Montano nodded. "What do you say we do a little snowshoeing today? Or maybe cross-country skiing?"

I bit my bottom lip. "I really need to write, but you can if you want."

"Nah, I was only offering so you didn't think I was lazy."

I looked him up and down, happy to be distracted by his well-toned body. "You don't look lazy."

He leaned over so his mouth was close to my ear, his breath hot on my neck. "Neither do you."

I offered to clean up when we were done eating, but Montano refused to let me. "Go write. I'm hoping if I'm a good enough boy, you'll let me read it."

"You'd have better luck if you were a bad boy," I answered, smacking his bottom as I left the kitchen.

An hour later, when my phone reminded me it was time to stand, I went looking for Montano, never expecting to find him doing yoga in the living room.

The view of his ass in the downward dog position was enough to make me drool. When he moved into a side plank, he caught me watching.

"Wanna join me?" he asked.

"I'm afraid if I do, I wouldn't get much writing done the rest of the day."

"Nah, yoga clears your mind and increases your creativity."

"Maybe another time." I returned to the bedroom and picked up my computer. Just *seeing* him do yoga increased my creativity plenty, and I couldn't wait to get more words on paper by way of a hot yoga-y sex scene.

When I heard the shower go on a few minutes later, I added that to the end of it. Only in both cases, my heroine wasn't sitting in front of a computer. She was enjoying everything I was only fantasizing about. Lucky girl.

I crossed my legs on the bed and squeezed my thighs together when I saw Montano come in with only a towel wrapped around the lower half of his body.

"I forgot to grab clean clothes."

"Do you want me to leave?"

He studied me long enough that I thought maybe I hadn't heard him answer and he was waiting for me to get up.

"I can go," he offered.

I smiled. "I'm curious. What has you so lost in thought?"

"Wondering what you're writing on the other side of that laptop."

"Hmmm."

"What?"

"I guess what we're thinking isn't that different. I was wondering what was on the other side of that towel."

"You show me yours, maybe I'll show you mine."

I shook a finger at him. "It doesn't work that way. No maybes, and we do it at the same time."

He laughed and walked out of the room, clothes in hand, leaving me feeling as unamused as frustrated.

Since he was done with his workout, I went out into the main room for a change of scenery. One reason I liked writing on my laptop was I could do it anywhere. I wasn't stuck in one room or even in my house. I could take it into the village and sit outside at a café, or if it was chilly, pick a corner table and watch the world go by as I drank my coffee or wine, ate cheese and fruit, and wrote my words.

I loved writing the places where the stories took me when I dove into them. That's why I traveled as much as I did. Each new place I visited became a possible setting for a future book. Whether it was a villa in the Italian countryside, a pensione in a village, or even an apartment in a city like Milan, a flat in London, a house in Munich, or a room in a boutique hotel in Salzburg.

Until this book, the one I never intended to write, none of them had been set on the East Coast of the United States. Funny, given it's where I grew up.

Since it was sunny, I thought about sitting out on the deck, but my laptop was running low on battery, so I decided to perch myself on the sofa instead.

19

Onyx

"Blanca is in the other room. Why do you ask?"

"We're running out of places to look," reported Diesel. "We've looked everywhere."

"According to her father, there is something at the camp that is imperative it be found. Keep looking."

"Do you think Blanca might have any ideas?"

"My guess is she'd do what you're doing, just not as thoroughly since it's what you're trained for."

"This is not what I was trained for."

Diesel Jacks was a language savant. At last count, he spoke twelve fluently. I'd read in a brief somewhere that he went to Cornell and graduated *summa cum laude*.

"It's an assignment you're perfectly capable of carrying out, Diesel. Get back at it and find whatever it is before I have to drive down there and do it for you."

He laughed. "Damn, you sounded like my dad just then. Doc and Fatale made the right choice putting you in charge of the new unit."

I'd been so wrapped up in Blanca, I hadn't given much thought to the new unit, K19 Shadow Operations. Admittedly, I liked the concept, and I agreed with Merrigan when she said that K19's core team had become too visible to be effective in missions where we suspected the bad guys were operating inside the intelligence community.

Rather than going out to where Blanca was, I opened my laptop and settled in where she'd been earlier—when she told me she was wondering what was on the other side of my towel.

If she were any other woman, I probably would've dropped it there and then, and let her see for herself. But the truth was, for the first time in my life, I didn't want any other woman to see me. I sure as hell wanted Blanca to, though. I wanted to see her too. All of her. How in the hell was I going to keep this wall I'd erected between us up? There'd never been anyone I felt such an immediate connection with. Especially not her sister. Sure, I'd felt an attraction, but that was so much different than really connecting with a person.

I wanted Blanca, and she wanted me, and I was old and wise enough to know it wasn't just physically. That meant I needed to get my ass back down to Canada

Lake and find whatever the evil bitch who'd tried to kill me left there.

I set my laptop aside and went into the other room. "How's writing going?" I asked.

"I'm enjoying this one."

"Don't you enjoy them all?"

"Some more than others."

"There's something I want to talk to you about," I said, sitting down beside her when she closed her computer and turned her body to make room for me on the sofa.

"I'm listening."

"The team back at the camp hasn't had any luck finding whatever it was your sister left there."

"And?"

"I'm going to head down there in the morning and see if I can help."

"You're going to?"

"Yes."

"Not me?"

"It will be safer if you stay here."

"Huh." Blanca got up, grabbed her laptop, went into the bedroom she'd originally been sleeping in, and slammed the door closed.

This was behavior I was used to. Not from her, from Sofia. The latter, I would've ignored until she got over whatever innocuous thing I had done to make her mad, even if it took days. Blanca, on the other hand, I couldn't ignore.

"Hey," I said, knocking on the door. "Can we talk about this?"

"You want to talk about it now?" I heard her ask.

"Uh, yeah."

The door flew open. "It would've been a better idea to talk about it prior to you making the decision to go look for something that is mine to find."

She tried to slam the door again, but I stood in the way. "Did you hear what I said? You'll be safer here."

"Did you hear what I said? Montano, whatever Sofia left is mine to find. In fact, I should be a lot angrier. The whole time you and your 'team' have been searching for something that doesn't belong to you."

"What are you doing?" I asked even though it was obvious she was packing.

"The rental car outside is in my name. As soon as I have my stuff together, I'll be getting in it and driving away from here."

"You have no concern whatsoever for your safety?"

Blanca threw the last of her stuff in her bag and zipped it up. "I figure that I'll be safe enough once I've gone home. I doubt anyone will follow me back to Italy. Would you please excuse me?"

I stood in the doorway with no intention of letting her pass. "You're wrong about someone following you to Italy. They'll follow you to Outer Mongolia if they think you have something that might incriminate them. That's what we think it is, Blanca. We believe your sister had enough on whoever she was working for, that she could use it to make sure they didn't try to kill her once she was no longer useful to them."

"She's dead."

"That's right."

"So they killed her anyway."

"I don't believe so."

"Are you saying the plane crash was an accident?"

"I don't believe the intended outcome was your sister's death."

"I don't like it when you talk that way. Like you're reciting from a manual."

"I'm stating facts—" I'd almost called her sis. "Blanca, please, let's not do this. I have two agendas:

to find what your father believed your sister left at the camp and keep you safe while I'm doing it."

She dropped her bag, plopped down on the end of the bed, and her eyes filled with tears.

Instead of staying in this room where her packed bag sat, I lifted her into my arms and carried her into the bedroom we'd shared last night.

I rested her body on the mattress and stretched out beside her. I brushed her tears away and stroked her hair. "Why are you crying?"

Blanca closed her eyes and shook her head.

"Neither of us is going anywhere, so you might as well tell me."

That made her open her eyes, if only to glare at me.

I leaned forward and kissed her. "Tell me why you're crying."

"It's stupid."

I pulled her over so her head rested on my chest. "Nothing that makes you cry is stupid, angel."

"I…" She couldn't get any more words out; her tears had turned into sobs.

I tightened my hold on her and soothed her the best I could. Eventually, her breathing evened out to the point I thought she may have fallen asleep. Moments later, she spoke.

"I wanted to believe that whatever she left behind was something for me. Something to mend what was broken between us. Now, that will never happen."

"I wanted to believe that too. Part of me still does."

"Then, you wouldn't find what you need."

"Neither would you."

She turned her face so she was looking at me. "How did my sister ever let you go?"

"It wasn't meant to be between her and me, Blanca. Meeting you has shown me that."

"Why?" she whispered.

I gripped the side of her face and kissed her, but she pulled away.

"Why?" she asked again.

"Because it was you I was supposed to meet."

"Montano—"

"It's true. Can you tell me you don't feel it? I've never felt this way with any other woman. *Never.* And truth be told, I didn't believe I ever would."

"No happily ever afters."

"No. Not for me. At least until I met you."

"We hardly know each other."

I kissed her again, and this time, she didn't try to pull away. "Blanca," I murmured between nuzzling her nose with mine, nipping and licking her lips. "You know that isn't true." I went in hard and deep, and almost sighed in relief when I felt her giving it right back to me.

"Montano," she said, pushing me against the mattress and climbing on top of me. "I want you."

"I want you too."

"But?"

"No butts, except this sweet one," I said, digging my fingers into the cheeks of her perfect ass.

"I want to have sex with you."

"I want to have sex with you too, angel."

"No lectures about how it's too soon or how we aren't ready for it?"

"No lectures," I answered, but in a voice no longer playful.

"What? Whatever it is, just say it."

I rolled us both so I was above her. "I don't want to have sex, Blanca. I want to make love to you, and you know as well as I do that neither of us is there yet."

The anger I'd seen in her eyes earlier returned. "I just said we hardly know each other, and you said I knew that wasn't true."

"There's a difference between not knowing each other and being ready for something that will change us forever." I brushed her lips with mine. "That's what I want, angel. The first time our bodies become one, I want to be ready for it to change my life forever." I stared into her eyes, waiting for another argument, but one never came.

"Let me go with you tomorrow. Don't leave me here alone."

"You wouldn't be alone. Wasp and—"

Blanca pressed her fingers against my lips. "If I'm not with you, I'm alone, Montano. Please, I'm begging you, take me with you."

"Okay."

"You promise? You aren't going to get up in the middle of the night and sneak off?"

"I wouldn't do that."

"Do you, uh, want me to go sleep in the other room?"

"Is that what you're going to do? Sleep?"

"Probably not right away. I'll write for a while."

"Where's your laptop?"

"In my bag."

"Don't go anywhere."

Blanca laughed. "You neither."

I grabbed her bag from the other room and switched off the lights. When I came back, Blanca was standing at the side of the bed. *Naked.*

20

Blanca

Montano dropped my bag with enough of a thud that, for a split second, I wondered if my laptop was okay. All thoughts of anything other than the man stalking toward me left my head.

"You…are…a…goddess," he moaned, standing in front of me and taking in every inch of my nakedness. He kissed my lips, my cheek, and down my neck before dropping to his knees in front of me.

Part of me expected him to leave or at least protest, but he did neither. He teased the nipple of one breast while his mouth toyed with the other. He snaked his arm around my waist and pulled me as close to him as I could get. He gave each breast equal attention before trailing his lips down the center of my body. With his free hand, he spread my legs and parted my folds with his tongue.

My fingers wove into his hair, helping me keep my balance as his mouth ravished my pussy. When I felt his long, thick finger breach my opening, I cried out, bending at the waist and moving my hands to his back.

I didn't have to plead or beg. Montano seemed to know exactly when I needed more and what of. When he added a second finger and the stiff tip of his tongue circled my clit, an orgasm tore through my body that I felt from the top of my head to my toes.

"Oh my God," I moaned, my knees going weak.

"Get on the bed."

"Not until you're naked too."

Montano smiled, pulled his shirt over his head in one swoop, and dropped his pants. I reached for his cock, but he grabbed my wrist before I could wrap my hand around it.

"You aren't going to let me touch you?"

"Oh, yeah, you're going to touch me, angel. But not until I let you."

"You're mean." When I stuck out my lower lip, Montano nipped it.

"You started this your way; I'm going to finish it mine."

Since the first thing he did upon finding me naked was give me pleasure, I decided it would be in my best interest to do things his way.

"On your stomach."

God, that growly voice of his put me right back on the brink of another climax. Or maybe it was the electrical current that flowed between our two bodies from the first moment we met. He'd asked me more than once if I'd felt the connection between us, and I sure as hell had.

He straddled my body so his hardness rested between the cheeks of my ass, but instinctively, I knew not to move, to take all the pleasure this man wanted to give me and not try to do anything to rush him.

When he moved my hair from my neck and scattered kisses down my spine, my body broke out in chill bumps and I shuddered. I could tell that brought a smile to his face.

I giggled when he bit first one and then the other cheek of my ass, and mewled in pleasure when I felt his finger thrust into my pussy. He held me still as he brought me to my second orgasm, this time with the fingers of his other hand pinching my clit.

"I knew it would be like this," I heard him murmur. "You're so responsive to me."

"Will you let me touch you now?" I asked, looking over my shoulder.

"I don't know. I'm still enjoying having my way with you."

Once again, Montano was every woman's ideal, more concerned with my pleasure than his own. The last person I wanted to think about was Sofia, but I couldn't help but wonder why she wouldn't have held onto this man forever.

As he made his way up my body, he kissed my side which, of course, was ticklish. When I squirmed and giggled, he used his tongue, which made me squirm and giggle more.

"I love your body," he whispered when his lips reached my neck.

I felt my muscles tense, unable to control the reflex brought on by his words. I expected him to roll away, but he did the opposite. He flipped me over and rested between my legs, holding his weight off my torso with his powerful arm.

"I love your body, Blanca."

"I would love to explore your body, Montano."

"I'm not going to let you get away with ignoring what I just said to you or your initial reaction to it."

"Really, it's fine to forget all about it. My reaction, that is."

Montano shook his head slowly. "I love *your* body, Blanca."

"Thank you."

"There are no memories in this room with us today."

I turned my head away. "We don't have to do this."

"We absolutely do."

"Montano, please. I don't want to talk about my sister when we are naked, bodies pressed together."

"You think I wanna talk about your sister?" He winked and I smiled. "It's you and me in this room. It's your body I can't get enough of, but more importantly, it's you, Blanca, that I can't get enough of. Someone told me once that when it's right, it's easy."

I smirked. "You think I'm easy?"

"See? That's what I mean. Even when we have something tough to talk about, we can smile through it. Make each other laugh, put each other at ease."

He was right. It was so easy to be with him. When I freaked out about him going to the camp without me, it was more that I didn't want to be here without him. It wasn't only that he made me feel safe. I would just miss him.

"That's better," he said, right before he brought his lips to mine. "Your body is softening, letting me sink into you. I'm going to say something, and I want you to promise me you'll remember I'm saying this to *you*."

"Okay."

"*No one's* body has ever felt as good to me as yours does."

"No one's has felt as good as yours either."

"See how easy that was?"

I looked into his eyes. "Can it really be this simple? Is it really possible to find someone who you can't find anything wrong with? I write it into my books, but can it actually happen in real life?"

He shifted his body so he was next to me, leaving me chilled. Within seconds—of course—he covered us both with a quilt.

"I'm ruining the sexy moment, aren't I?"

"I'm not going anywhere, angel. I just didn't want to crush you when my arm went to sleep."

"You're too perfect to be real."

"Far, far from it."

I turned on my side and propped my head on my hand. "So, that was all about my pleasure? Nothing for you?"

"You're crazy if you think I didn't enjoy myself."

"But don't you want…more?" I trailed my fingers down the side of his body, but for the second time, he grabbed my wrist and stopped me.

"There is something I want," he said, turning to face me.

"What?"

"I want us to write a sex scene for your book together."

I shuddered when a zing of pleasure went straight from his words to my pussy. "Oh my God, I almost had another orgasm just then."

"See?" he said like he had earlier. "It would be hot, right?"

"Scorchingly so."

"There's just one thing. I don't know what fancy words you use to write this stuff, but it has to be a scene where they both experience outrageous pleasure but without having intercourse."

I raised a brow. "Why not?"

"Because they aren't ready to take that step."

I rolled my eyes and sat up. "How do you want to do this?"

"I have no idea. You're the writer."

"Okay, then, I'll write the woman's point of view, and you write the man's."

"Couldn't I just tell you, and you do the writing? If I do it, it'll sound stupid."

"There isn't a writer alive who hasn't thought that, writing their first sex scene. Or their one hundredth."

21

Onyx

Blanca got off the bed and pulled her laptop out of the bag that I'd dropped on the floor when I walked in and found her naked.

"Did I break it?"

When she got back on the bed and opened the lid, I was relieved to see the screen light up.

"I'm going to write my part, and then we'll do yours."

"Oh."

"You can read over my shoulder if you want."

"I want." As I watched, Blanca wrote in exact order and detail, everything I had just done to her, but in a way that made it sound so fucking sexy I had to grab my cock.

"Oh no, you don't," she said, grabbing my wrist like I'd done to her. "If I can't touch it, neither can you."

If I weren't so turned on I couldn't think, I might've laughed. Right now, though, I needed *someone* to touch my cock. I wriggled my wrist out of her clutches. "Put your hand around it, but just for, like, thirty seconds. Give it a hard squeeze."

"Are you writing your part now?"

"God, that sounded awful, didn't it? No, wait. Let me start again. But now you can't touch me yet."

"Before we go any further, answer me this. Will I ever get to touch you?"

"Oh, yeah."

"Good. Now let's get started."

"How?"

"Close your eyes and imagine everything our heroine would do to our hero that would bring him outrageous pleasure."

I loved that Blanca used the words I had.

"Let me read yours again just to get my mind in the right place."

She rolled her eyes but handed me her laptop.

"How about this? What if I write it, and then you fix it?"

"We can give that a try. Just try not to overthink it. We'll consider this a first draft."

I typed out the absolute most rudimentary, ridiculous sentences, referencing her words over and over again.

By the time the hero got off, I was close to it myself, and that was without either of us touching my cock.

"Ready to let me read it?"

"Maybe. I don't know. Give me a minute." I read it over again, all the while imagining that whatever the woman did to the guy was really Blanca doing it to me. I took a deep breath when I finished and handed her the laptop. The second I did, I wanted to grab it back.

She closed the lid and turned her body to face me. "I want you to know that what you're feeling right now is the same way I feel whenever I let the first person read something I've just written."

"Terrified?"

She smiled. "Absolutely. But more like I just ripped my chest open and invited someone to stomp all over my heart."

I couldn't help but rub my chest. "Ouch."

"It usually doesn't hurt. Unless what I've written is crap. But that's the level of vulnerability."

"Shit," I muttered, shaking my head. "How do you keep doing it?"

"That's a good question. Mainly because I can't not do it. If that makes sense. I have to write. At least for now. I'm not sure I'll always feel that way, but if I go too long without doing it, my fingers hurt."

"Seriously?"

She shrugged. "That's the best way I can put it." Blanca put her hands on the laptop and looked into my eyes. "Ready?"

"As I'll ever be."

I read while she did. When she squirmed and mewled, I took it as a good sign. When she brought her own hand to her breast and toyed with her nipple, almost absentmindedly, I wanted to rip the laptop out of her hands and fuck her senseless.

"This is good," she said, not taking her eyes off the screen. "I really like this part."

"Which part?"

Instead of pointing to the screen, she moved it out of my grasp and closed it. "What we need to do now is make sure this would all work in real life."

"God, I was hoping you'd say that."

After setting the laptop on the floor, Blanca tore the quilt that covered our bodies away.

"Hmm, let me see if I can remember how this went." She straddled me, and I could feel the wet heat of her pussy on my stomach. She raised both my arms.

"Hands here, and do not let go," she said as I gripped the headboard. "If you do, I'll stop."

I swear my eyes rolled back in my head when she improvised that part.

"You don't mind if I edit a bit as we go, do you?"

I shook my head, unable to speak.

Just like I'd written, Blanca brought her mouth to mine and kissed me hard, angling her head and thrusting her tongue deep into my mouth. I could feel her nipples harden when her breasts brushed my chest.

She moved from my mouth to my neck and put her tongue in my ear. The reason I'd added it to what I wrote was because the first woman I ever kissed had done that to me and I fucking loved it.

Moving down my body, Blanca flicked my nipple with her tongue while the index finger of her other hand swirled around the areola of the other. When she scooted down a little more and her wetness brushed against my cock, I thought about changing the rules I'd put into place. If she positioned herself to take me inside her, I wouldn't last even a minute.

Instead, she continued acting out my words. The anticipation of knowing what she was about to do was mind-blowing. When she swirled her tongue around the tip of my cock, I clutched the rails of the headboard, so thankful she'd given me something to hold onto.

When she took me into her mouth, I was sure I'd finally died and gone to heaven. As if she were following a script, Blanca cupped my balls and looked up at me. When my eyes met hers, I spoke the words I'd written. "Deeper, angel."

When she took me into her throat, I moved my hands to her hair. "Blanca, baby, stop."

She shook her head. My back arched, and I groaned, my cock pulsing inside her mouth.

The entirety of my body shook as I came down from the *outrageous* pleasure she'd given me.

"God-all-fucking-mighty." I rested my head against the pillow and wove my fingers in her hair. She licked her way back up my body and brought her mouth to mine. I gripped the side of her face and kissed her with more passion than I'd ever kissed anyone. "That was incredible."

She smiled. "You wrote it. I think it worked pretty well."

"That was about a thousand times better than what I wrote. Damn, how do you write that stuff and not… you know…do something about it?"

She laughed. "Most of the time, I'm anxious just to get through it, if you want to know the truth. I'm also imagining characters in my head, not myself, and that makes it very different."

"How is it different? Aren't your characters just an extension of you?"

She cocked her head. "How would that work with the guys?"

I laughed. "Right. I guess it wouldn't."

"It isn't the case with the women either. I mean, all my characters are different. I tell their stories, not my own."

"Are you saying your real-life sex life isn't racier than the *Fifty Shades* stuff?"

"My real-life sex life has been lacking."

That made me a damned happy asshole. I reached out and covered her breast with my hand. Before I could do the same with my mouth, she scooted away from me.

"If you start again, I'm not going to be happy when you stop." She twined her fingers with mine. "I know that if we did have 'intercourse' as you put it, I would regret it. I understand everything you've said about both of us not being ready for that. But I can't lie, Montano; I've never wanted a man more than I want you."

"Do you want me to sleep in the other room?" I asked.

"Would you rather I did?"

"Hell, no."

"Same. Besides, isn't it, like, six in the evening?"

I looked over my shoulder at the clock on the bedside table. "Five thirty."

"Is there any of that food left from last night?"

"I'm sorry, angel, I snacked on most of it. There might be some bread and cheese left. On the other hand, there's still stuff on the menu we didn't order last night."

"You better handle the ordering this time so I don't overdo it quite so much."

I don't know if it was because I was starving or I just wanted to make Blanca feel better about the night before, but I ordered just as much food as she had, plus dessert.

22

Blanca

I waited until Montano's mouth was full before saying the thing I'd been holding in since we sat down to eat. "I need to ask you something that will probably be difficult for you to answer, but I have to do it anyway."

Montano's eyes scrunched, and he continued chewing on a forkful of Wagyu beef tartare. "Okay," he muttered before taking a second bite.

"You're kinda the perfect guy."

He smiled. "What's with the 'kinda' shit, angel?"

I laughed. "Okay. The perfect guy."

"Should I wait for your question, or am I good to move on to the next course?" He was eyeing the roasted beet salad I'd been drooling over.

I mean, how could I not? Beets on top of baby greens with orange and grapefruit segments, drunken goat cheese—whatever that was—and an apple-balsamic dressing.

"Blanca? Question?" he asked, setting his fork on the side of his plate.

"When I asked this before, you said you wouldn't answer, because Sofia wasn't here to tell her side of the story, but I just can't understand how she let you go."

I watched while he thought about what I'd just said, wondering if he'd make a joke about it.

He took a deep breath and leaned forward, resting his arm on the table. "That first day when you 'accidentally' showed up on Thanksgiving?"

I rolled my eyes and sighed. "Yes."

"You said something about how I might've been your brother-in-law."

"I remember."

"I said I wouldn't have been."

I nodded, knowing exactly what he was talking about. I'd been stunned by his quick and emphatic response.

"Sofia and I often had differing opinions about things. Maybe if we hadn't worked together, we could've overcome some of them, but I doubt it."

"She was headstrong."

"Damn straight."

He was thoughtful again, but I didn't push. Whatever he was about to say, I sensed was difficult for him.

"A few months before she died, your sister was taken hostage on an op that took a bad turn. In the end, she was rescued, but more and more, I wonder if what happened affected her more than she ever let on."

"Was she hurt?"

Montano nodded. "She was beaten up pretty bad. Suffered a concussion, but that was the worst of it— physically anyway. She was bruised and sore, ended up spending a night in the hospital. The next day, I took her back to South Carolina. I figured she'd want to see your dad, but when we arrived, she said she wanted to go straight to her condo. At the time, I just assumed she wouldn't want him to see her that way. Wouldn't want to worry him."

"Makes sense."

"She didn't want me to stay with her."

"Did you anyway?"

"Nope." He took a bite of the salad, giving me time to think about what he'd said.

My sister—the pilot—was taken hostage? It was the first time it hit home that Sofia and Montano working together, or maybe who they worked for, was a lot more involved than I'd originally thought.

"Why'd you ask if I stayed with her anyway?"

I shrugged. "I don't know. I guess that if it were me, you wouldn't take no for an answer."

"You're right. You're very different than your sister." He reached over and stroked the back of my hand with his fingertip. "I mean, are any twins really *that* much alike? My mom and her sister have lived next door to each other most of their lives, and they're nothing alike. Except they're equally competitive."

"I don't know any other twins to say one way or another. I'm honestly struggling with this very question as it relates to Sofia and me."

"Just because two people look identical doesn't mean what's inside is. A couple of guys I work with are married to twins. I don't know either of the women that well, but they seem very different. One is outgoing and the other is shy."

"It used to frustrate me when people compared me to Sofia. It probably frustrated her too."

"Not hungry?" he asked, perhaps noticing I hadn't taken more than a couple of bites.

"I don't know. I just have so many unanswered questions, and at the same time, I'm not sure I want to know a lot of it."

23

Onyx

This was it. Blanca was giving me an easy lead-in to tell her what had really happened with her sister and that I knew more than anyone did about how Sofia died. Yes, it had been in a plane crash, but from what I'd been told, Halo's shot killed her instantly.

Your sister was a double agent. We don't know for how long, we don't know for who, and we definitely don't know why. On top of that, her intention the day she died had been to kill me. Only, I survived and she didn't.

Which part of that would hurt Blanca the most? That her twin was a traitor who'd betrayed her country? Or that I had kept this information as long as I had?

It would be easy to tell myself I was hesitating to give her more information until we learned what Sofia had been involved in and how deep her betrayal went. That was a lie. I wasn't telling her, because I was afraid that once I did, she'd never forgive me.

Even how much I'd left out of the story about the op when Sofia was kidnapped would probably infuriate her. But how much of that could I really divulge?

The night Sofia was taken hostage was a culmination of a years-long mission during which Special Agent Malin Kilbourne, the very same agent who'd told Blanca how to find me, took down one of the dirtiest directors in the history of the Central Intelligence Agency. It wasn't just him. Several members of the then-executive administration were either arrested or, in the president's case, impeached and forced to resign from office.

That Sofia ended up a pawn in the end game was my fault. We were on the Central Coast of California, not far from my parents' place, for a meeting of the K19 Security Solutions partners. Since Sofia hadn't yet been extended a partnership offer, she wasn't invited. I suggested she spend some time at the beach, and once the meetings—and the mission, which I was not permitted to read her in on—concluded, I would join her.

She didn't understand why she couldn't just stay on the ranch where this was all taking place and simply not attend. When I hemmed and hawed, she flew into a rage, accusing me of lying to her. She hadn't been wrong.

The short helicopter ride from the ranch to Cambria, where I'd stayed in the days following Thanksgiving, was short but tension filled. There was nothing I could say or do that would make her less angry. My hands were tied—metaphorically.

The next time I saw her, Sofia's hands were literally tied. As I'd told Blanca, she'd been severely beaten by the very man who Malin ended up taking down, the one who knew she'd never give in, never tell him what she knew in order to protect her own life. She would, however, feed him every bit of information he wanted in order to spare Sofia's.

It hadn't mattered. Doc Butler's father, a man known in the intelligence world as Burns, had surveillance in the wine caves on the estate where Malin and Sofia were being held. It allowed us to find and rescue them as well as get everything needed to prove the director and his accomplices were dirty.

Until I told Blanca the short version of what happened to her sister during that mission, I don't think I'd realized the kind of lasting impact it had on her. Had that been the turning point? Had my betrayal, at least in her eyes, and the torture she'd suffered because of it, made her turn against not only me, but her country? I'd never know for certain.

"I'm sorry."

I raised my head and looked into Blanca's eyes. "You have nothing to be sorry for."

"I've ruined what was an amazing afternoon. Not to mention, you aren't eating much more than I am."

"You know what I'd really like to do?"

Blanca raised a brow. "Do tell?"

"I want to go back into that bedroom and fall asleep with you in my arms."

"I'd like that too."

We cleaned up the kitchen, took turns with our night-time routines, and got into bed, saying very little else.

"Are we heading back today?" Blanca asked the following morning when I brought a latte to her in bed.

"Yes."

"Both of us?"

"Yes, angel. Both of us."

Less than an hour later, we were on the road.

"Can we change the subject?" Blanca asked thirty minutes into our silent drive.

I smiled. "What would you like to talk about?"

"Pleasant memories."

"I'm all for that." I only hoped she didn't ask me to share very many about my relationship with her sister. "What are your favorites from your time at Canada Lake?"

Blanca rested her head against the back of the seat, and a look I could only call serene came over her face.

"So many things. Playing cards, like I told you before. Sherman's, though, is definitely up there."

"The amusement park?"

She nodded. "It felt like we spent every night there during the summer. Either my parents would give us a ride or one of the other kids' parents would."

"Jimmy Messick's?" I snarled.

"Oh my God. Yes. Jimmy Messick's. Anyway, Sofia and I had our favorite rides, very different ones as you might imagine."

"What was yours?"

She looked at me like I should know the answer. I shrugged.

"The carousel. Duh."

"And Sofia's?"

"The Whip-it."

I couldn't stop myself from laughing out loud. "What in the world is a Whip-it?"

"It's a ride that went around in an oval, kind of like a roller rink. We sat in cars attached to metal beams. On the straightaway, the cars would pick up speed and then whip around the end."

"Doesn't sound like that much fun."

"I wonder how many kids ended up with arthritis later in life because of that ride." She tapped her lower lip. "Anyway, as soon as we got there, Sofia would run to the end of the midway to the Whip-it and I'd dash off in the direction of the carousel."

"Leaving Jimmy in the dust? I'm liking this story better."

"Ha, ha. No, I didn't leave Jimmy in the dust. He'd come along, not that he was with us every night, and hang out until he got bored. Then he'd make me go on the Ferris wheel with him." She shuddered.

"Not a fan?"

"I didn't mind it so much. When it would stop at the top, there was a view of all of the lake. The camps would be lit up, and the water shone with the reflection of the colorful lights."

"Why'd you squirm?"

"Jimmy used to like to rock the seat. It made me so nervous."

"See? He was a jerk."

Blanca laughed and looked away. She was quiet for a while, and I let her get lost in her thoughts.

"It's where I started writing," she murmured.

"Really? At the amusement park?"

"At the carousel. I'd sit on one of the horses and go around a few times, and then I'd sit on one of the seats that didn't move, pull out my notebook, and write."

"What would you write about?"

"Remember that movie, um, Julie Andrews was in it, and so was Dick Van Dyke?"

"Vaguely."

"There was a scene in it where they were at a park, riding the carousel with the kids Julie Andrews nannied. In the movie, the horses turned into animation and rode away with Julie, Dick, and the kids on their backs. I don't think they went far, but in my stories, I did."

"Like where?"

"Everywhere. Paris, London, Madrid, St. Louis."

"Wait. St. Louis?"

"'Meet Me in St Louis' was my mother's favorite movie. At Christmas, we'd watch it over and over again. I remember wishing I could surprise her and take her there one day."

"On horseback?"

"You're hysterical," she deadpanned. She looked to her side as we approached the Canada Lake store. "We're back already? Wow. Can we stop and get sandwiches? I'm starving."

I was too, but even if I weren't, I'd grant every wish of the charming, beguiling, gorgeous, intelligent, creative woman sitting next to me. Even if it was to take her to the moon.

Like we did the first time, we ordered different types of sandwiches, promising to share once we got to the camp.

"Since the electricity wasn't really out, can I stay in my own camp tonight?"

"There are a couple stipulations."

"Oh yeah?"

I nodded. "First, remember your camp is not winterized. If my feet get too cold, we're moving over to Ranger's camp."

"Your feet?"

"That's the other stipulation. You have to let me stay there with you."

"Done."

We ended up sleeping at Ranger's camp because, as I'd predicted, her camp was too cold. Even the team that had been searching the place, along with Wasp and Cowboy who'd returned with us, took turns sleeping at another cabin that had been winterized.

The next morning dawned sunny and warm, so after a hearty breakfast prepared by Ranger, we went next door to start our version of the search.

"Are you sure your people actually looked?" Blanca asked after I'd lit the wood stove and it warmed enough that we didn't have to stand right in front of it. "Nothing is out of place."

"Training," I mumbled when a feeling of impending doom settled on me. I wondered if it was the same as what Blanca had experienced our first day here. I wanted to clear the rooms of the cabin, but I didn't want Blanca coming with me, nor did I want to leave her here by the stove.

"Come with me," I said, motioning to the front door.

"Where am I going?"

"Back to Ranger's."

She opened her mouth, then closed it.

"Trust me, okay?"

"Of course."

Once there, I texted Diesel and asked him to have the team meet me at Blanca's camp.

When he arrived with Swan, Trap, Wasp, and Cowboy, I had them do a full sweep of the entire camp, the outside perimeter, and run a check for surveillance. They didn't find anything, but that didn't make my feeling go away.

All clear to bring Blanca over, I texted Ranger.

"Everything okay?" she asked, coming in the door.

"If it weren't, you wouldn't be here," I said with a wink. "I'd like to formally introduce you to the team. This is Diesel Jacks, Swan Lee, and Trap Flannery." I pointed to each one. "You already know Wasp and Cowboy." I turned to Diesel. "You can decide who stays and who goes. We don't need all of you here."

"Roger that," he responded, motioning them out to the porch.

"Be right back," I told her, joining them. There was something I wanted set up, and Diesel would need Ranger's help making it happen.

"Where are you?" I hollered when I came inside and didn't see or hear Blanca.

"In the loft."

I took the stairs two at a time and found her on the floor near an old trunk. "Find anything?" I asked, noticing she'd pulled several things out and was looking through them.

"Not anything significant. Just memories."

I sat on the floor beside her. "That is the reason you're here."

She looked at me and cocked her head.

"That was your original plan, right? Come here and see if you could 'connect' with your sister over happy memories?"

"You're right. I guess I lost sight of that."

For the next hour, Blanca went through the contents of the trunk. Some things she commented on, others she didn't. Every once in a while, I'd catch a tear roll down her cheek. Once she was done looking at whatever it was, I'd do my own check. I wasn't looking at memories, though. I was looking for something Sofia might have left for her—or us—to find.

"Time for a break," I said when we finished combing over everything in the loft and didn't find anything. I'd also received a text from Ranger saying what I'd asked him to take care of was done.

"Where are we going?" Blanca asked, following me outside and over to the rental SUV.

"I'm in the mood for ice cream."

"If you're thinking about Sherman's, I doubt it will be open. I'm sure it was a fluke when we found it open the day we went. Given that bus full of kids showed up, maybe the school made arrangements for a field trip."

"Let's go look anyway."

She rolled her eyes but got in the car without further argument.

"You were right," I said, pulling into the parking lot and trying to sound disappointed, even though I'd already known it was closed.

"Hey, look! The doors of the dance hall are open."

While that wasn't part of my plan, anything that made Blanca that excited brought a smile to my face. "Wanna go check it out?"

"Are you kidding? Of course I do." She was out of the car and racing toward the building before I'd even cut the engine, much in the same way she had the day we got ice cream. Watching her, it was easy to imagine her as a kid or teenager when her parents would drop her off. Her reaction was that of unbridled joy, and I loved seeing and experiencing it firsthand.

"Wow," I gasped, walking into the building that looked like it had been frozen in time.

On the first floor, there was an old-fashioned-looking counter and soda fountain, several rows of Skee-Ball machines, and other arcade-type games that looked as though someone had been playing them just yesterday.

As we ventured farther inside, there was an area filled with picnic tables. While the windows were boarded up, it was easy to imagine them all open and the breeze coming off the lake, keeping the now-freezing room cool.

Regardless of where we went, the floor we walked on was made of creaky wooden planks that any home remodel company would likely have paid a fortune for.

"I'm going to take a peek upstairs."

Blanca hadn't seen him yet, but the man I'd made arrangements to meet there was standing just outside and gave me a head nod.

While she ran, I walked up the staircase made of the same wooden planks as the floor, hoping no one else ventured in here and saw the same dollar signs I did. It would be a shame to have this place dismantled and sold off for the restoration hardware inside.

One side of the second floor was empty but for a stage, a bar, and high-top tables situated near more of the boarded-up windows. On the other side, there was additional table-seating, fancier than what was below.

"My parents and their friends loved coming here on Saturday nights. In the summer, bands played Friday nights and Sunday afternoons too, but Saturday was when everyone showed up." She stood in the middle of the floor and spun in a circle. "Sofia and I would check in with them every couple of hours, and our dad would order us Shirley Temples."

I walked over to where she was and held out my hand. When she put hers in it, I pulled her close, hummed what I knew would be familiar to her, and we danced.

Soon, she sang the words to my melody and I joined her. There was no more appropriate tune to consider "our song," at least for me. Blanca Descanso was under my skin and would remain there for the rest of my life. I had no doubt about it.

Whether she would want to remain a part of it once she learned the truth of what I'd been keeping from her, remained to be seen. Still, I knew I'd never forget her or the way being with her made me feel.

"Watching my mom and dad is what made me want to write romance books." She bit her bottom lip, and her cheeks flushed. "I took it a bit further than that, but back then, I couldn't imagine two people being more in love."

"Tell me about them."

"My favorite thing about my mom was how easily she laughed. She had a wicked dry sense of humor and didn't shy away from off-color jokes." A smile lit up Blanca's face. "She was also so loving. Even though Germans aren't known to be that demonstrative, she was. If I sat beside her, she'd put her arm around me or stroke my hair or hold my hand. My dad was affectionate too, but with my mom, it was as though the words she didn't say out loud were conveyed through her touch." Her eyes met mine. "That probably doesn't make sense."

"It makes perfect sense to me." Every touch, every look, every smile, every eye roll made me fall in love with Blanca just a little bit more. Yes, I loved her. That I'd known her for a couple of weeks didn't matter. It wasn't just that she was under my skin; I loved her heart and soul.

Funny how people in love say that when you meet "the one," it feels different from any time before, when they thought they'd met their soulmate. I completely got that now. With what I thought was my dying breath, I'd told her twin the sentiment, but I hadn't meant it. At least not the same way. Maybe part of me loved Sofia, but not at all in the same way I loved Blanca.

Afraid I'd say the words that would make me look ridiculous, I pulled her into my arms and kissed her.

"What was that for?"

"You're magnificent."

She pulled back, and the smile left her face.

"That's a good thing, Blanca."

She appeared stunned and shook her head.

"What? What did I say to upset you?"

"I'm not upset. It's just that my father used to say that to my mother."

"And I bet she was."

Blanca took one more long look around. "We should probably get going before someone finds us in here. I wonder why it was open."

"Maybe someone's doing maintenance."

We walked down the stairs and out onto the midway, where I hoped Blanca would notice her surprise. She didn't disappoint me.

"Look!" she exclaimed like she had when we arrived and she saw the dance hall was open. "The carousel is running." She took my hand and pulled me along with her as she raced toward it.

"Well, hello there," said the man we'd met the night we went to the Outlet restaurant. Al, as he'd told us then, had lived all seventy-seven years of his life here, and at one time, had been the general manager of the amusement park. "Wanna take a ride?"

"Are you serious? I'd loved to," said Blanca, climbing on the platform and walking between the rows. "This one was my favorite." She climbed up on a white horse that was adorned with pink-painted flowers and ribbons.

We stayed on long enough that I was dizzy and slightly nauseated, but there was no way I'd spoil a single minute of her fun.

"We should probably let the man get on with whatever he was doing."

"Isn't there something else you want to do?" I asked, motioning to Al to stop the ride.

"I don't know. What?"

I climbed off my horse, held out my hand to help her down, and led her over to one of the stationary seats. Once we sat down, Al started the ride up again.

"My sister used to make fun of me every chance she got, but this was the one thing she never teased me about. In fact, one year, she got me a music box that was a carousel horse. I don't know how she found it, but it played the same tune this one does."

"How old were you?"

"Hmm. Early teens, I think." Blanca's eyes opened wide, and she grabbed my hand. "The music box!"

"What about it?"

"It's at the camp! I found it and put it in my suitcase when I first got there. Right before I got the weird feeling and ran out."

"Stop the ride," I shouted at Al.

"Everything okay?" he asked, walking toward us as it slowed down.

"Something we have to check on back at the camp," I told him. "But thank you for this."

"My pleasure. Sure felt good to see this baby back in motion."

"Wait. You arranged this?" Blanca's eyes filled with tears, and I pulled her into my arms. "You are such a good man, Montano Yáñez."

Her words both warmed and chilled me. Soon enough, Blanca would learn I wasn't a good man, and when I finally braved up enough to tell her the truth, she wouldn't think so either.

24

Blanca

I felt the air chill as we walked from the carousel to the car, and it had nothing to do with the temperature. It was as though the heat emanating from Montano's body shut off. Even his hand that held mine felt cold.

"Are you okay?" I asked once we were in the car and on our way to the camp.

"I'm fine. How about you?" he responded without looking at me.

It was such an odd response for him that I didn't know what else to say. He didn't appear to notice when I didn't answer.

When we arrived, I didn't wait for him to come around and open my door. I got out and raced toward the camp, anxious to get to the music box before he did. I had no idea why I felt as though I needed to. It was just instinctual.

"Do not go inside without me, Blanca," he called after me. "It may not be safe."

I couldn't decide which to listen to: my own gut reaction or the pleading tone in his voice. I sighed and took a step back from the door.

"Thank you. Now, please wait out here with Ranger." I hadn't seen the other man approach. "Where did you put it?"

I couldn't bring myself to tell him. "It's mine."

Montano put his hands on my shoulders. "I have no intention of taking your music box. I just need to see if what we believe your sister hid is inside it."

While there was no good reason for me to, I started to cry.

"Blanca, please." He tightened the hold he had on my shoulders. "You have no idea how important this might be."

I had no idea how important it *might be* to him? Did he have any idea how important it *was* to me? "Inside the left pocket of my suitcase," I muttered.

Without another word, he raced inside. Moments later, he came out with my music box and rushed toward the other camp.

My head was spinning. It was as though once Montano had it in his hands, I became so inconsequential. He didn't even look at me.

"Wait!" I shouted, running after him. I grabbed his arm, and when I did, my precious carousel horse fell to the ground, breaking into pieces.

"There it is," I heard Montano say as though he'd just seen the Holy Grail or some other priceless treasure. He reached out, plucked the tiny piece of cardboard that looked like a SIM card for a cell phone out of what was left of the only thing my sister had given me that ever mattered. "Blanca, I'm so sorry. I—"

Ranger bent down beside me. "Onyx, I've got this. Now go!"

25

Onyx

"Go and help Ranger with Blanca," I barked at Wasp when I stormed into the other camp and found him in the kitchen.

"What's going on?" he asked.

I spun around on him. "Follow orders!" I shouted.

"What the hell?" said Diesel, whom Wasp had been talking to.

"This," I said, setting the SD card on the counter. "We need to see what's on it." When I handed it to him, Diesel took it over to the laptop that sat on the kitchen counter.

"It's password-protected," he said, taking it out and handing it back to me.

I'd expected it to be. "We need to get it to the cryptologists at agency headquarters. I don't want to fuck around with it here. Find Trap and have him arrange for the fastest mode of transport he can." For the first time since this mission began, I was glad Money had sent him in.

"I'm right here," I heard him say.

"Good, then, you heard me." I pulled out my phone to alert Money we were on our way, but froze when I heard a gun cock. I looked up and saw Trap's trained on me.

"What the hell?" I muttered, repeating Diesel's words from a minute ago.

"Weapons, boys," he said, waving his gun between Diesel and me. "On the counter."

I held up one hand, reached behind me, grabbed my gun, and slid it over to him. Diesel did the same.

"Hand it over."

Diesel looked at me, and I looked at him.

"I heard you!" Trap bellowed. "I know one of you has it."

Rather than respond, I engaged. "Trap, what in the hell are you doing?"

"Just give me the card, Onyx."

"What the fuck, Trap? Were you working with Corazón?"

"Corazón worked *for* me. Just like the rest of you should have."

"For you? How would that have played out? Were you planning on taking over K19? I doubt Doc would have gone along with that. Razor or Gunner either."

Perspiration broke out on Trap's upper lip, his breathing accelerated, and his eyes were like lasers on mine. "You think it's a goddamn joke, but I could've done the job better than any one of the assholes it was given to. Dutch, Striker, and Money, for fuck's sake. He's a piece-of-shit analyst."

"You didn't get the job you wanted, so you betrayed your country and became a double agent?" I said in a taunting tone of voice.

"Shut up! Hand the card over before I kill you."

I glanced over at Diesel.

"It's still in the computer."

"How did Corazón fit into all this?" I asked as I watched Trap grappling with what to do next.

"Pilots stick together. She understood how little value we were to the government. You use us like machines and then toss us to the curb. You tell us to go drive a fucking bus where we don't make as much as we did when we were active duty. She figured that out early. Hell, she was barely out of flight training before we onboarded her."

"I'm a pilot."

"Were." Trap waved his gun at Diesel. "Get the card out and give it to me."

"So it was the money? Is that why the two of you sold out your country? The almighty dollar?"

"Says the guy who is probably collecting a multimillion-dollar settlement from the same government who doesn't want to pay us shit."

"What's on the card, Trap? Did Corazón leave an insurance policy in case you betrayed her?"

"She was an amateur, never measured up. It was only about the money to her. No loyalty that way. I guess you realized that before we did. Did us a favor, taking her out. It won't be long now until I do what she failed to."

In the split second I heard a gunshot ring out from next door, I leaped toward the counter and my gun. Before I could reach it, I felt a bullet tear into my back and something hard and heavy come down on my head.

When I came to, I was on a medevac chopper and Diesel was seated beside me. "Blanca?" I gasped.

I didn't hear his answer; everything faded to black.

26

Onyx
Christmas Day
Last Year
Washington, DC

I opened my eyes and looked up at my mother. Tears streamed down her face. *"Es un milagro,"* she exclaimed, putting her palms on my cheeks. *"Es un milagro de Navidad!"*

"Good morning," said my sister Erlinda, who was crying as hard or harder than my mother. "And merry Christmas!"

I tried to speak, but my throat was too dry and scratchy.

Someone I didn't recognize but who had to be a nurse based on her attire, burst through the door, followed by my oldest brother, Carlos.

"Welcome back, Mister Yáñez. I'm Peggy, and I'm your nurse today." She checked my IV, the monitors, and looked into my eyes. "I've heard you have the most beautiful hazel eyes. It's nice to finally see them."

"Water," I gasped.

"Only a few sips to start with." She brought a cup and straw to my lips.

"Where…am…I?" Damn, it hurt to talk.

"George Washington University Hospital. Can you tell me your name?"

"Onyx."

"Is that your first name?"

"Montano."

"That's right. I won't ask if you know what day it is."

"Christmas," I said anyway, looking around the room at my mother, brother, and sister. "What happened?"

"From what I understand, you were in a plane crash. You've been in a coma for twenty-seven days."

I closed my eyes. A plane crash? I didn't remember anything about a plane crash.

"Where's Monk?" I asked. I couldn't remember much of anything except dreaming that he was talking to me—endlessly.

Erlinda moved closer when the nurse walked to the other side of the room. "Do you want us to call him?"

"That bastard has been talking my ears off."

"He's been here every day," Carlos told me. "I swear there were times he stayed all night too."

I rested my head against the pillow and closed my eyes.

"What, did you go back to sleep?"

"Being awake is exhausting." When I opened my eyes, my family was gone, but Monk was there. A woman stood behind him. "Is that Saylor with you?"

"It's so good to see you," she said, walking closer to the bed. "Merry Christmas."

"Merry Christmas, and it's good to be seen." I reached out my hand to her. "He's talked about you nonstop." I motioned to Monk.

"Yeah?"

"He told me to hurry and wake the fuck up so he could go home."

"Nice," muttered Monk, shaking his head.

"Tell her it isn't true," I chided.

"She knows it is."

I motioned for him to get closer, and when he did, I grasped his hand. "You kept me alive, son."

"You did that all on your own. And, by the way, I'm older than you are."

I smiled. "In age maybe, but certainly not in wisdom."

"We should go. Let some of your family get back in here," he said, his eyes filling with tears.

I refused to loosen my grasp on his hand. "You are my family. You're my brother. Even if you are a pain in the ass."

"I'll be back in the morning."

I shook my head. "Take the day off, son. You've earned it."

He shook his head.

"I'll instruct the nurses not to let you in."

"They won't listen. They like me."

"Give me an hour, and they'll like me better." I looked over at Saylor and winked. "Keep him in bed all day tomorrow."

"It would be my pleasure," she answered, returning my wink.

Monk squeezed my hand. "I'll see you soon."

"I have a feeling I'll be here a while."

"As will I."

***

Four months. That's how long I'd been in this fucking hospital, trying to piece my life back together—the life that Sofia Descanso had ripped to shreds.

No one would tell me why the plane I was flying crashed. The therapist that came to see me once a day, whether I acknowledged his presence or not, insisted I allow the memories to come back on their own.

They were there, in my nightmares anyway, but in bits and pieces. The day I woke up in a cold sweat and found Monk where he always was, by my side, I looked at him in horror. "She shot me?"

He nodded and then told me as much as he knew, saying he didn't give a shit whether the therapist or anyone else approved.

"We're going to miss you, Mr. Yáñez," said the head rehab nurse.

"No offense, Steph, but I'm not gonna miss this place."

"No offense taken. We all wish you the absolute best."

Hospital policy was that patients were to be taken to the front door in a wheelchair, but as hard as I'd worked in the last four months to walk again, no one mentioned policy.

For now, I was headed to the loft Monk had been living in since I arrived at the hospital back in November. Considering I had no idea what I was going to do with the rest of my life, it was easy to say yes when he offered to let me move in with him.

"Nice place," I said when he unlocked the door. "Surprised you didn't spend more time here."

He opened the refrigerator and handed me a beer. "This is you," he said, motioning to the master bedroom.

"I'm not taking your room, son."

"I don't sleep in there."

"Why not?"

"Just don't."

I threw my bag on the bed and kicked off my shoes. "Goddamn, it's gonna feel good not to have someone waking me up all the damned time to take my blood pressure. You aren't gonna do that, are you?"

"Fuck, no," he said, going back out into the kitchen and pulling food out of the refrigerator. I followed.

"All right, son, why the hell does that big ol' bed in there sit empty every night?"

"It just does."

"What happened between you and Saylor?"

"Didn't work out."

"Tell you what. I'll make a deal with you."

"Not interested."

I laughed. "You don't know what I'm going to say."

"We aren't gonna do this tonight."

"Here's my offer. I'll tell you what happened with Corazón if you tell me what happened with Saylor. If you don't agree to this, there ain't anybody ever gonna know what happened in that fuckin' cockpit."

While Monk had told me what he learned from Halo and Tackle, the other two guys that survived the plane crash that should've killed us all, no one knew what else I remembered about that day. Monk hadn't pushed, but I knew damn well he wanted to. He wasn't the only one either.

In the last four months, the founding partners of K19 had all visited me at the hospital on a semi-regular basis. Like Monk, Doc Butler and his wife, Merrigan, the managing partners, hadn't pushed. My guess was that Doc wanted to, but Merrigan wouldn't let him.

Even Gunner Godet, who had less sensitivity than a single-cell organism, skirted around asking me what I remembered and dropped it when I gave him a halfassed answer.

The one other thing no one asked me about, or even brought up, was when I planned to get back to work.

Monk, the only person whose shit I put up with, didn't give me any the day the team of doctors responsible for overseeing my recovery gave me the worst news of my life.

I didn't remember most of what they said; only certain words stood out as I listened to them tell me I had better odds of being struck by lightning than being cleared to fly again.

As far as I was concerned, I died the day they told me I'd never get my wings back. Work? Who the fuck cared? The only thing I'd ever wanted to do had been taken away from me by the woman I'd called my heart.

27

Onyx

"Where in the hell am I?" I asked when I came to again and saw Monk sitting at my bedside.

"George Washington University Hospital."

"What the fuck is going on?" I tried to sit up, but restraints were holding me down. "Get these off me!" I shouted.

"Mister Yáñez, you must calm down," said a nurse rushing in when my movement set off the bed alarms.

I looked at Monk, whose focus was over my shoulder. I followed his gaze in time to see another nurse inject something into my IV port. "Fuck," I muttered as I slipped back under.

I raised my head. "Monk?"

"Yeah?"

"Am I dead?"

He looked over his shoulder at the monitor measuring my heartbeat. "Nope."

"Why am I back here?"

"You were shot."

Fuck. Again? I closed my eyes and rested my head against the pillow, trying my damnedest to remember what had happened. The last thing I could recall was being in the Adirondacks and finding something Corazón had hidden in Blanca's music box. *Blanca.*

I raised my head again. "Monk?"

He leaned forward. "Yeah?"

"Where is Blanca?"

"Onyx, she's—"

I held up my hand. "Before you say another word, I'm warning you. If you tell me anything other than that she's fine and safe, I won't…I won't…" I couldn't go on.

"She's fine and safe."

"Thank God." I released my grip on the bed rail, realizing then that I wasn't tied down. "They took the restraints off?"

"When you came to before, you were less than an hour out of surgery."

"Surgery?" I looked down at my legs. I couldn't feel either one of them.

"It's the epidural. It'll wear off in a couple of hours once they stop it," said Monk, following my line of sight.

"What are you doing here?"

"I didn't feel like sitting through the hotwash. They can brief us together later."

I'd meant in DC, but whatever. Monk always answered the question he wanted to, even if it wasn't the one asked.

"What happened to Trap?"

"Dead."

"Who shot me?"

"Hatchet."

"Are you going to make me keep asking questions?"

"You're the one firing them at me."

"Tell me as much as you know."

"It isn't a lot."

"Monk, I swear to fucking God—"

"If you'd shut up for a minute, I'd tell you."

I glared at him but didn't speak.

"According to Ranger, you left Blanca and him outside when you went into the cabin his family owns."

"I remember that much."

"He was helping her clean something up when Wasp came out the door you'd gone in and motioned Ranger toward the boathouse, mouthing at him to move out."

"He must've seen someone."

"Affirmative. Ranger said within minutes, he heard a shot ring out that sounded as though it came from behind the other cabin. Seconds after that, he heard two shots in close succession come from inside his place."

"Who'd the first shot take down?"

"Hellcat. Swan got her."

I recognized the name of the woman we'd believed was working with Hatchet and who we'd seen on surveillance casing Ranger's camp.

"Hatchet dropped you with the second shot right as Wasp fired at him. If Wasp hadn't, Hatchet's aim might've been better. As it was, he just missed your spine."

Just missed my spine? *Fuck.*

"You're gonna be fine," said Monk, answering my unasked question.

"What about Trap?"

"With all the commotion, Diesel was easily able to take him out."

"Back to Blanca. Where is she?"

"That part, I'm not sure about."

"But you know she's safe?"

"Yes. She's safe. She was relocated so she stayed that way."

The door opened, and Ranger walked in. "You're awake."

"Is it over?" Monk asked him before I could respond.

"For the most part. Descanso wasn't exactly a cipher expert, so it didn't take the cryptologist long to get in and start assembling the report. We're reconvening in the morning, though."

"How long have I been here?" I asked.

"About seven hours," answered Monk.

"How long have you been here?"

"Five."

My eyes scrunched, and I looked from him to Ranger.

"Diesel alerted him from the Medevac that you were being transported."

Adrenaline crash, coming out of anesthesia, physical and emotional exhaustion—I couldn't say for sure what it was that made me tear up, knowing Monk had gotten on the first flight he could and came straight here. He would've had to in order to be here almost as long as I had.

28

Blanca

"What is going on?" I cried when I heard a gunshot.

"Just stay down for me, okay, Blanca?"

I covered my ears and closed my eyes tight when I heard two more. "God, please let Montano be safe," I prayed silently.

Things remained quiet for too long, but soon, I could hear people shouting, just not what they were saying. Seconds later it seemed, there was what sounded like a train roaring in our direction.

"What is that?" I shouted.

Ranger, who had been watching the whole time through a small window with his gun drawn, knelt down beside me. "Medevac helicopter."

"Who is it for?"

"I don't know."

"What's going on?" I asked for the second time.

He stood. "We're waiting for an all-clear."

I remained crouched down, eyes shut tight, hands over my ears, silently praying again and again for Montano's safety.

When the noise from the helicopter faded until I could no longer hear it, Ranger knelt down again. "Let's go," he said, helping me to my feet. "Are you okay?" he asked when one of my legs went out from under me.

"It's asleep."

"We'll wait a minute."

I nodded my head a few seconds later, and he opened the door to the boathouse. The woman I recognized as Swan was walking toward us.

Her eyes met Ranger's, but neither spoke as they led me to a vehicle I didn't recognize.

"Where are you taking me?" I asked when Swan opened the back passenger door and I saw Cowboy behind the wheel.

"Somewhere safe," she said, motioning for me to scoot over and getting in next to me.

Neither she nor Cowboy said another word as we drove away from the lake.

After more than an hour, we approached an airport. "I'm leaving?" I asked.

"We both are."

Cowboy pulled up to a curb, Swan got out, and I followed. I watched him get two suitcases out of the trunk. One was mine.

"Wait," I said when he went to the front of the car. "Where is Montano?" His eyes met Swan's, and neither spoke.

I wrapped my arms around my waist and raised my chin. "I'm not going anywhere until you answer me."

"Come with me," said Swan, gently pulling my arm, but I refused to budge. "Once we're inside, I'll tell you what I know."

I nodded and followed, looking over my shoulder in time to see Cowboy drive away.

Rather than going through the main part of the airport, she led me through back corridors until we came to a secured location. "It'll just be a minute," she said, looking at her phone.

"You said you'd tell me what you know about Montano."

"Onyx was shot and is being transported to a hospital, where he'll undergo surgery."

God, no. It couldn't be. He was shot because of me. Because my sister left something in our camp that I was intended to find. This was all my fault—and Sofia's. If Montano died…I couldn't allow myself to think about that possibility. "Do you have any idea of his condition?"

"I do not."

"I heard more than one gunshot."

"The others don't matter."

"What does that mean?"

"They're dead."

29

Onyx

"This is highly unorthodox," said a nurse I didn't recognize when Ranger came in, pushing a cart holding a desktop computer and two laptops, and instructed her to leave.

"Not the first time we've heard that," Monk muttered.

"I know you wanted to skip this, but they're insisting," Ranger said to him.

"What?" I asked.

"Debrief."

Ranger fiddled with the computer he'd set in front of me, and Money McTiernan's image came on the screen.

"Onyx, good to see you," he said when Ranger activated my audio and video and I watched the screen populate with more images, including those of the two men in the room with me.

"McTiernan," I responded. "You're going to change your mind once you hear what I have to say. In fact, I don't think you belong in this meeting."

"Onyx, Doc here." McTiernan's image minimized, and Doc's became the largest on the screen. I could see Merrigan seated beside him.

"I can see you."

"Good," he said at the same time Merrigan said hello.

"Hey, Fatale," I answered.

Doc shifted so the screen's focus was on her. "If it's all right with you, I'll be facilitating this meeting."

"Of course."

"Very well, let's get started."

There was a knock on the door; Ranger stood, unlocked it, and slipped out. He returned and locked it again. "Sorry," he mumbled, regaining his seat. "There won't be further interruptions."

"Thank you, Ranger," said Merrigan, clearing her throat. "Late last night, Doc and I received the brief outlining what was found on Descanso's SD card. Between then and now, several security measures have been put in place, including the members of the K19 team, as well as their families, being transported to multiple secure locations."

"*Jesus,*" I said under my breath.

"Precisely," Merrigan responded.

I nodded and she continued.

"First, we have proof that Flannery and Descanso were working for United Russia and have been for quite some time. As we do not yet know the extent of UR's remaining network of double agents, we will be operating with the highest degree of caution until further notice."

While Trap hadn't admitted who his employer was, the news did not surprise me. Merrigan's next words, though, shocked me to my core.

"Most urgently, we learned there exists a specific list of individuals UR has targeted for assassination, at the top of which are Doc and I."

My eyes opened wide.

"It is not, however, limited to us. In fact, all the partners are on the list as well as many of our contractors."

I could see Gunner, Razor, and Eighty-eight, the other three founding partners of K19, nodding their heads.

Merrigan's voice increased in volume, and she leaned closer to the screen. "I can assure you we have already begun formulating a response to this information and will be backed by the full force of the US and UK governments along with several members of NATO and the United Nations. In other words, we are calling UR out on the world stage and intend to make them pay dearly for this."

My mind reeled with what she was saying, but there was only one question I desperately wanted the answer to, and I was having a damned hard time waiting. I looked over at Ranger and Monk and then back at the screen.

"Fatale? I'm sorry to interrupt—"

"She's somewhere safe, Onyx. I give you my word. For your safety and hers, we're keeping that location secret. Our only goal at this time is to make sure everyone associated with K19 remains alive."

I closed my eyes and turned my head when my eyes filled with tears of relief at her confirmation of what Monk had told me last night.

Merrigan continued the briefing with what she referred to as the highlights of the information Sofia had accumulated during her career as a double agent.

Flannery was not the only name within the report I recognized as still being with the CIA. But with each agent Merrigan named, my anger at Money increased to the point where I was ready to exit the meeting.

"God-fucking-dammit," I muttered under my breath, looking away.

"Onyx? Do you have something to say?" Merrigan asked.

"It can wait."

Money's image became primary on my screen. "I was unaware of Trap's—"

"Stop right there," I shouted, sitting up and banging my fist on the cart that held the computer. "You were fucking out of line in sending him in. Because of your interference, my life, as well as those of the other agents on *my* team, was in danger. I stand by what I said earlier. You don't belong in this meeting."

"Money didn't send Trap in," I heard Merrigan say. "He was not aware of Trap's involvement. Given this op was *ours*, he followed *our* protocols."

"Meaning what? Are you calling my actions into question?"

"Onyx, please," I heard Merrigan say right before Monk pulled the power plug on my computer.

"You, out!" He pointed at an open-mouthed Ranger. *"This is the very reason I requested a second-level briefing!"* he shouted as loudly as I had at Merrigan.

Ranger looked at me and, when I nodded, left the room.

"You okay, bro?" I asked Monk, who was pacing near the window.

He stopped and glared at me. "No, I'm not okay. Are you okay?"

"I think I'm better than you are."

"Fucking assholes," I heard him mutter as he reached into a bag, pulled out a flask, and held it out to me.

"You better go first."

30

Blanca

"Welcome aboard," said Wasp when Swan escorted me up the steps and onto a private airplane. Toward the back, I saw Cowboy stand and walk in my direction.

"What's going on?"

Wasp looked at Swan.

"I was not given the authority to brief her."

Wasp stepped out of the entry to the cockpit. "Go ahead and get settled," he said to her while motioning me in the other direction. "Have a seat."

"No, I will not *have a seat.* Not until someone tells me what's going on. *Right now, Wasp!"*

"I'm sorry. I thought Swan would've done that already."

"She didn't."

"I do think this would be easier if you took a seat."

"Montano?" My eyes filled with tears, and I covered my mouth with my hand.

"He's in surgery, but the doctors have said his injuries from the gunshot are not life-threatening."

Knowing that much, I sat.

"As you know, we recovered the SD card your sister left hidden in your music box. Someone is currently trying to gain access to whatever she put on it. Until we know more, we're acting on the assumption that you remain in danger. Consequently, we've been instructed to transport you to a secure location."

"Where?"

"California."

"Where is Montano?"

Wasp looked at Cowboy.

"Not in California," he answered.

"Why can't I be with him?" Was the reason I was being taken to the opposite coast because he'd requested it?

"A decision needed to be made quickly regarding your relocation. At the time, we did not know the details of Onyx's condition."

"You said his injuries aren't life-threatening."

"That's right." Wasp rested his hand on my arm. "I know this is difficult, and I know it's hard to understand.

Please trust that we're doing what we believe is best for everyone, at least for the time being."

"I have no choice, do I?"

"I'm sorry, Blanca."

By the time we landed, it was dark and there were no immediate landmarks to identify where we were. All I knew was that we were close to the ocean.

I remained seated until Wasp and Swan came out of the cockpit.

Wasp leaned on the arm of the seat beside me. "I know this is a lot to take in, but I understand you visited Onyx's family recently, is that right?"

"Yes. On Thanksgiving."

"If it's any comfort, where we're going is very near there. It's a place owned by the family of one of the founders of the company we work for. By we, I mean, myself, Cowboy, Swan, and Onyx. Ranger works for him too. Our boss' name is Doc Butler."

"Okay."

"It's called Butler Ranch, and you'll be safe there."

I remembered seeing it when I stayed at Los Caballeros and said so.

"See?" said Wasp. "It's right next door."

If he thought that was somehow comforting, he was wrong. I'd been flown across country with no say as to whether I wanted to go after being told I was in danger, and without being able to speak to the only person in this world I thought I could trust.

There wasn't anyone or anything that would give me comfort unless Montano was waiting wherever they were taking me, and that, I knew, was impossible.

By the end of the night, I had to admit I'd been both right and wrong. I was right in knowing Montano wouldn't be here waiting for me. Wrong in thinking there was no one or nothing else that could comfort me.

When we pulled through the ranch gates, an inexplicable sense of peace settled over me. It was more than the moonlight illuminating the vineyards. I could only describe it as a feeling opposite of what I'd felt the day I walked into the camp on Canada Lake and knew within minutes I had to get out. When Cowboy pulled up to the main house and cut the engine, I couldn't wait to go inside.

Wasp got out, opened the back door, and held his hand out to me. "You're going to love Mr. and Mrs. Butler. They're, like, everyone's favorite grandparents," he said, leading me up the porch steps.

The front door opened, and two people younger than what I'd expected came out.

"Doc!" said Wasp. "I didn't know you'd be here."

"That's the idea," the man answered, stepping forward to greet me. "Blanca, I'm Doc Butler, and this is my wife, Merrigan. Welcome to Butler Ranch."

"Laird, she's here," I heard a woman with a Scottish brogue shout out from inside the house.

"Hello," I said when the woman Doc introduced stepped forward too. Instead of shaking my hand, she pulled me into an embrace. "This must be very hard for you. Please know we understand and will answer whatever questions we're able to."

A woman much closer to the age I was expecting came out the door. "There's the lass," she said, rushing toward me. "You must be Blanca." She tucked her arm through mine and led me inside. "I'm Sorcha, and this is my husband, Laird."

"Give the girl some space to breathe, Sorcha," the man said, approaching us. "Welcome to our home."

"It's very kind of you to allow me to stay here. I hope I'm not intruding." More than intruding, my main concern was that if I were in danger, now they were too.

"You'll be staying in the cottage that used to belong to our son Maddox. He and his wife, Alex, have their own estate and winery now," Sorcha explained. "You'll have plenty of privacy when you want it, and when you don't, just come to the main house, and you'll have the company you're craving."

I looked over at Merrigan, who was smiling indulgently at the older woman. "Kade and I will help her get settled."

"Are you hungry, dear?" Sorcha asked.

"I'm not, but thank you."

Wasp and Cowboy were speaking with Merrigan's husband near the front door when she led me in that direction.

"We're on our way out, but you're in good hands here," said Wasp.

"Thank you for all you've done for me. Both of you," I said, looking from him to Cowboy. "And please convey my thanks to Swan as well." I had to admit I wasn't disappointed when she didn't deboard the plane and come with us.

Merrigan showed me around the "cottage" that was larger than any home I'd ever lived in while Doc fetched my bag.

We were in the kitchen when he came inside. "Can I get either of you ladies anything?" he asked, walking over to the refrigerator that I saw was well stocked when he opened the door.

"I'll have a glass of chardonnay," Merrigan answered. "Blanca?"

"I'd like one too, please."

"Let's sit in the other room."

Given that I'd downed half my wine before Merrigan and I sat in the living room, I appreciated it when Doc filled my glass a second time before sitting as well.

"As I said earlier, Doc and I will do our best to answer whatever questions you may have."

"I wouldn't know where to start. Although, I do have a concern about my being here."

"Go on."

"Wasp told me you believe I'm in danger."

"We do."

"My question, then, is, why would you bring me to your parents' home? They seem like such lovely people." I stopped talking when a look passed between the two. They were both smiling, which unnerved me more.

Doc looked over at me and, perhaps noticing my scowl, cleared his throat. "I'll explain."

I took another sip of wine.

"Onyx shared with us that he informed you some about what we do?"

"He said my sister worked for you."

"That's right," said Merrigan.

"You caught the look that passed between my wife and me when you mentioned how lovely my parents are. You're absolutely right. They are the nicest, most caring people I know. They're also former intelligence operatives themselves."

"Quite formidable ones, in fact," Merrigan added.

"While my mother is retired, my father is still quite active in the business. There are few better in the world at what he does."

"Few?" teased Merrigan.

"Okay, maybe one, and even that is questionable."

Doc looked directly at me. "The point is for you to understand that you are not compromising their safety by being here. The truth of the matter is, there are few safer places in the world for them and for you."

"While Doc and I do not know what your relationship with Onyx is and are not asking you share that with us, I sense you are very worried about him."

"I am."

"I promise you we will keep you posted on his condition as we know more."

"Will I be able to talk to him?"

Merrigan looked at her husband and then at me. "Not at this time," she answered.

31

Onyx

"You ready to get out of here?" Monk asked the following day when he walked in not much after dawn.

"Have you spent so much time here they finally just made you a doctor?"

He glared at me. "I'm leaving in an hour."

"Yeah? Goin' home, son?"

"Or somewhere like it."

"Give Saylor my best."

Monk nodded.

"Thanks for coming."

"Only way I see you anymore is if you're tied to a bed in a hospital."

I put my hand on my heart. "Ah, Monk, have you missed me?"

"Stay away from people with guns," he said, patting my shoulder.

"Probably won't be a problem since I'm sure I'll be looking for a new career field."

"You and me both."

I hadn't heard from Merrigan or anyone else from K19 after he pulled the plug on the computer I was using, and I doubted he had either.

"See ya, Onyx."

"See ya, Monk."

He wasn't gone five minutes before Ranger came in.

"Are you here to say goodbye too?"

He cocked his head. "I'm your transport."

"Yeah? Where to?"

"Orders are we're going back to the camp, and we'll have company."

For a split second, I got my hopes up, but I quickly realized he meant we'd have backup.

"The surveillance team has already been there. They stripped everything that was there, not knowing if it was something we installed or Trap had. The new system is supposed to be fully functional by the close of business today."

"Who's paying for all this?"

"What do you mean? K19 is."

"Yeah, you still work for them?"

Ranger shook his head.

"Now I feel bad. They fired you, bro? That ain't right. Don't you worry. I'll get it sorted out. What happened yesterday is on Monk and me."

"It's on Monk, not you, but no, they didn't fire me."

"You quit? What did you go and do that for?"

"If I didn't know better, I'd swear Hatchet's bullet got you in the head, not your back."

I rubbed the right side of my scalp. "I do have a pretty big lump where somebody hit me."

"Shit. I forgot about that. I'll quit jokin' around now. I don't work for them, because I work for you, Onyx. Haven't you heard? I'm second-in-command."

I shook my head. "Prepare to take over the reins, bro."

"Not happening. If you leave, I'll follow."

"Yeah? You gonna open that fishing-charter-boat business with me down in the Keys?"

"Sounds pretty damn good right now."

It was after ten before I got word that I was discharged and could go "home." Like the last time I left this hospital, I didn't stick around waiting for a wheelchair. I got dressed and walked out like I owned the damned place. Considering how much money this hospital raked in after keeping me here five months, I was probably getting close to being a majority stakeholder.

A black SUV was waiting at the entrance; Wasp got out of the front passenger seat when we approached. "Shotgun, or do you want to get some work done?"

"Neither," I said, opening the back door myself and climbing in.

Ranger went around the other side and, after getting in, handed me a laptop. "You've got some reading to do, boss."

"You can go first."

"I've read it already," he said, turning his head and looking out the other window.

"I don't want to, do I?"

"Better to just get it over with."

After skimming the brief that was over a hundred pages of shit I wished I never knew, I went back and poured over the details of Sofia Descanso's life as a double agent. The part that hurt the worst and made me feel like a complete asshole, was that our meeting was in no way accidental. The only thing I was thankful for was that I wasn't the person who'd brought her to K19.

If that had been the case, the burden of guilt would've consumed me.

As it was, she came to the team by way of an outfit K19 had worked with in the past, who supplied referrals for flight crews. Given her background check and references were impeccable, no one had looked twice.

I had no doubt that anyone coming into the organization in the future would experience a vetting like none of us had seen before.

"Hey, uh, I just got a text from my brother."

Evidently, today was my day to have to hear about shit I'd rather not. "And?"

"He needs a place to stay."

"And?" I repeated, this time with emphasis that I hoped came across as *I really don't give a fuck.*

"Would it be a problem if he stayed at the camp?"

"What's his security clearance?"

"Top secret."

"Are you shittin' me?"

"I'm not. He's a data and systems engineer."

"Run it by the boss."

"Do you mean…"

"I mean Fatale, bro."

***

My family was used to me being in the midst of missions on Christmas, even when I couldn't get word to them, like this year. I felt guilty as hell, though, that Ranger and Jimmy weren't able to spend the holiday with their family. Jimmy could have, but when his brother told him we were essentially on lockdown, he said he'd be happier hanging with us anyway.

Wouldn't it just fucking figure that Jimmy Messick was the kind of guy that after you met him, he was impossible to hate.

Like his younger brother, Jimmy was smart, funny, a total bro. That he was going through a messy divorce sucked major balls, especially since he had two young kids. I had a feeling his soon-to-be ex was giving him a hard time about seeing those kids, which made his decision about Christmas an easier one to make.

It had been three weeks since I left the hospital in Washington, DC, and went back to the camp where everywhere I looked, I was reminded of Blanca. I tried my hardest to remember the fun times we had and push away the memory of her tears the day I broke her music box.

"How's it coming along?" Jimmy asked, joining me in the kitchen where I was painstakingly trying to piece the carousel horse back together.

I looked up at him and shrugged. "There's a problem." Before he could ask, I put the key in the bottom, wound it up, and set it back on the counter.

"Oh, man," he said, cringing. "That's pitiful."

It was bad enough that I couldn't get the horse to move up and down on its pole like it had before it broke, but the tune it played sounded like a horror movie track.

"Have you contacted the guy who made it?"

"What are you talking about?"

"The guy who owns the carousel company."

Since Jimmy was rarely obtuse, whatever he was trying to tell me had to be obvious. I just wasn't following. "Do you know how to get in touch with him?"

"Yeah, Al. I thought you knew him. You got him to open the ride for Blanca."

It figured that Jimmy knew the story. "Does he know how to get in touch with whoever made this thing?" I asked, pointing to the music box that had become my obsession.

Jimmy laughed. "*He* made that thing."

I shook my head. "I wish I knew what the hell you were talking about."

Ranger walked in. "What are you goin' on about, bro?"

"Al Jones."

"What about him?"

Jimmy walked to the fridge and pulled out a beer. "I don't know who needs this more, but since there's only one cold one left, I'm taking it." He popped it open and took a swig. "Al Jones of the Jones Carousel Company. His family has owned it for three generations. I heard Maisie is taking it over. She'd be the fourth, or fifth, I guess."

I looked over at Ranger. Something about what Jimmy said put the biggest smile I'd ever seen on his face—the one he quickly tried to mask.

"Are you saying Al's family built the carousel at Sherman's?"

Jimmy shook his head. "Not only that, Al's grandfather was Sherman Jones. You know, *Sherman*."

How did I not know any of this? The bigger question was, how come Blanca didn't?

"He made those too," Jimmy said, pointing at the music box I held little hope would ever work again.

"Not very many, though. I think he only released one a year."

"I had no idea," Ranger muttered.

"You weren't here as much as I was, growing up. Most of the kids who summered here got jobs either at Sherman's or the Canada Lake store. This one"—Jimmy pointed at his brother—"was always in some high school sport. It was either football, baseball, or track."

"I played basketball too."

"Helluva lotta good that did him. So, who's gonna call Al, me?"

"I can call him," said Ranger, pulling out his phone. Jimmy turned so his brother couldn't see him, winked, and gave me a thumbs-up. I had no idea what that meant, but it appeared I'd find out soon enough since two minutes later, Ranger announced we'd been invited over to the Jones' camp for dinner.

The minute we walked in, I caught on.

"Hi, I'm Maisie Ann. I'm Al's granddaughter. Come on in."

"I'm Montano, but most people call me Onyx." I stepped forward and shook her hand.

"Hey, Maisie. I don't know if you remember me—"

"Ranger Messick, how could I ever forget you? There wasn't a girl in Fulton County who didn't have a crush on you." Maisie turned to Jimmy. "Except Blanca Descanso, that is."

Jimmy laughed and walked straight in to talk to Al. When Ranger gave me a slight head nod, I followed.

"That sure was a romantic thing you did for your girl," said Al's wife, Mary. "I told my husband he should take lessons from you."

"I'm confused," said Maisie, walking in with her arm through Ranger's. "Grandpa said you were with Blanca."

"That's right. Stole her clean away from Jimmy." I nudged him with my elbow.

"But aren't you married?" she asked him.

"Separated, but as far as Blanca is concerned, I haven't seen her since I graduated from high school."

"How did you meet her?" Maisie asked me.

"I knew her sister."

"Oh. Um, what was her name again?"

"Sofia."

"That's right."

By the purse of her lips, I gathered her opinion of Blanca's twin was about the same as most everyone else in the area.

"She got a bad rap, that one," said Al. "But I'll tell you what; she worked her bottom off for me one summer in order to earn enough money to buy her sister one of those carousel music boxes." Al looked at me. "Ranger said something happened to it."

When I took it out of the bag and set it on the dining room table, Mary gasped. "Oh, it's worse than I imagined."

"You don't know the half of it," I said, winding it up.

"I see what you mean," said Al, picking it up and popping something off the bottom. Whatever he did, made the music stop. Thank God.

"Any advice?"

"Well, let me see." Al put on a pair of glasses and held the horse up to the light. "If you mean to fix it, no."

"Do I have any other options?"

Al shook his head. "These have become quite the collector's items. No two were alike. You could try going on one of those auction sites and see if anybody's got one for sale."

"I was afraid you were going to say that."

"Yeah? Already looked?"

The astronomical price people were asking for them was certainly a deterrent. However, the bigger problem for me was that none of the ones being offered looked anything like the one Sofia had given Blanca. "This was her favorite horse to ride on the carousel."

Mary and her granddaughter walked over to Al, each putting an arm through one of his.

"Gramps, please."

"Al, you know you have to. Think about what he did for her."

Al shook his head. "Even if I wanted to, I couldn't make another one." He held up his hands. "Arthritis is too bad."

"Maybe Onyx could help," suggested Jimmy.

I wasn't sure what he was volunteering me for, but based on Al's assessment of my repair job, I doubted he'd go for it.

Al's eyes scrunched, and he studied me for what felt like several minutes but was probably less than sixty seconds.

"Come with me," he finally said.

32

Blanca

I couldn't remember the last time I'd had a decent writing streak—one that was more than a thousand words. That wasn't exactly true. I'd written more than that, but they were all shit and I deleted them, so they didn't count.

Every day, I'd sit down with my laptop, determined to start a new book. Within hours, I'd abandon it. There was one book I couldn't let go of, though, and I'd tried.

I lost count of the number of times I'd dragged the story Montano and I started together to the computer's trash, only to recover it seconds later in sheer panic that it was gone forever. The fact I had backups didn't seem to assuage my fear that one day I'd open my laptop and it would somehow be gone.

It had been three weeks and two days since I laid eyes on Montano Yáñez. Twenty-three days since the best and worst time of my life ended. A little longer since I gave my heart to a man who would hold it forever, whether I ever saw him again or not.

I still didn't understand why I couldn't talk to him, unless, like I'd assumed before, he made the request that I didn't.

It was especially hard on Christmas and New Year's Day. It came and went in the same way they did every year for me, except this year, I spent most of the day thinking about Montano.

I told Sorcha that since my mother died, I hadn't celebrated any holidays. She and Laird still insisted I come up to the main house to eat with them. On both occasions, the warmth and sheer size of their family overwhelmed me.

Still another three weeks passed with no word on how long I'd be here. When Doc, whose name I learned from Sorcha was Kade, and Merrigan were last at the ranch, they said it wouldn't be much longer. However, they gave no indication of what that meant specifically.

They were also vague about when I might be able to talk to Montano. Maybe it was time I admitted to myself that he didn't want anything to do with me and move on.

I had, finally, been able to access what Laird had told me was an iron-clad network in order to notify my editor that my next three books would be delayed, as well as log on to make sure the auto-payments on all my bills were going through okay.

Today, like most days, I sat at the kitchen table of the cottage the Butlers had so graciously ensconced me in, doing nothing more than stare at my blank computer screen and think about Montano.

At some point, Sorcha would stop in to see me, using the excuse that she needed to make sure the refrigerator was stocked with everything I needed. When she came by yesterday, she told me she'd have a special surprise for me today. I hoped it wasn't food. My clothes were getting too tight as it was.

It was midafternoon and I had just finished deleting yet another book begun without meaning, when I heard her knock at my door. I almost wept when I saw Montano's mother standing with her.

"Please come in," I said, stepping out of the doorway. "Esmeralda, it's so nice to see you."

The woman pulled me into an embrace that felt like it lasted minutes. Truth be told, I never wanted her to let me go.

"Has something happened?" I asked, seeing tears stream down her cheeks.

"No, lass, everything is fine. She's just happy to see you," said Sorcha, patting my cheek. "We have some very good news, in fact." Sorcha motioned toward the kitchen, the place where we sat whenever she stopped over to chat.

She checked to make sure the teakettle had water in it, lit the fire on the stove, and opened the refrigerator. "You didn't eat last night, my dear?"

"I fell asleep, and when I woke up, it was too late to eat."

She shook her head. "You'll waste away to nothing. I'll bring more biscuits over later."

Considering she'd plated a half dozen for the three of us and there were still that many left, I hoped she didn't. It was a miracle that I'd been able to resist eating more of them yesterday.

Along with the flaky, buttery goodies, she brought butter and jam to the table.

"Sorcha, sit now," said Esmeralda. "We want to tell Blanca the good news."

"I'll just get the tea." When the kettle boiled, she added the steaming water to the teapot and sat down.

"I've heard from my Kade that you'll soon be able to go home."

I'm sure neither woman expected my reaction, given the look of horror on their faces when I burst into tears.

"I don't think those are tears of happiness," Sorcha said to Montano's mother, who put her hand on my arm.

"I don't think they are, either."

"Sorry," I said, getting up to wipe my face. "I've been so emotional lately."

"Mm-hmm." Both women looked skeptical.

"What will you do?" Esmeralda asked as I tried to keep more tears from falling and answer the one question I wasn't prepared to.

I shrugged. "Like you said, go home, I guess."

"Where is home, lass?"

"I've spent the last several years living in Italy."

"Ah, but that is not the question she asked, is it?" said Montano's mother.

"I don't have any family in the States," I half-heartedly explained. "I own property in New York State that I intend to sell."

"Why not live there?"

"It's a camp, err, cabin in the Adirondack Mountains."

"Sounds like a lovely place to live," said Sorcha. "Esmeralda, do you know our Blanca is a writer?"

I'd shared that information with Sorcha but no details about the types of books I wrote.

"Are you working on a book now?" Montano's mother asked.

"I am, and it happens to be set in the same place my camp is."

"What kind of book is it?"

"Um, romance."

Sorcha raised her eyebrows, and the two women smiled.

"Then, you must go back there and finish it."

"I don't need to. I often write stories in locations where I haven't been in a while. It isn't necessary for me to be in a particular place when I write."

"In this case, it is, lass."

I studied Sorcha, whose gaze remained on mine. She spoke with such certainty. How was it a woman who'd known me such a short amount of time could have such a strong opinion?

"You said your sister passed. Were the two of you close?"

Again, I was on the brink of tears. "Not at all, and the one thing I had—"

"What?" both women asked.

"It's silly."

Sorcha squeezed my hand. "I doubt anything that affects you in such a way is silly."

"Near the place where my family spent summers, there was an amusement park we used to go to. It had a carousel—" A sob tore through my chest, and both Sorcha's and Esmeralda's eyes filled with tears.

"Go on, lass."

I got up again, blew my nose, and sat back down. "It was my favorite ride. Anyway, for Christmas one year, my twin sister gave me a music box that looked just like the horse I always rode when we were kids."

"What happened to it, dear?" Esmeralda asked.

"It broke, and now it's gone, and it was the only thing I had to remind me my sister loved me. At least at one time in our lives."

Montano's mother sat back in her chair and let out a deep sigh. "As I told you when you were with our family for Thanksgiving, I understand your feelings more than most."

"Aye, you and Lucia are twins," said Sorcha.

"When we were young girls, no one fought as hard together as we did, but I always knew she loved me."

"I wish I could say the same."

"You can, dear. It doesn't matter whether you no longer have the gift itself. It's the memory of it that matters most. That, you will always have."

"She speaks the truth, lass."

"You're so young. How did your sister die?" Esmeralda asked.

"She was in a plane crash."

A look passed between her and Sorcha that I didn't understand.

"What?"

Sorcha used the pie server to put a biscuit on a plate and then added butter and jam to the side. "Here," she said, handing it to me. "You need to eat."

I was hungry after skipping dinner last night and not eating anything this morning, so I didn't argue.

"What do you think, Esmeralda? When she leaves should she return to Italy or the…what did you call it?"

"A camp. It's a cabin, but that's what they call them in that area."

"She must return to the camp. There is no question."

"Why? I mean, that chapter of my life is over. I don't see what good could come of it. I've made Italy my home."

Esmeralda leaned forward and looked into my eyes. "Nothing is over, Blanca. It's only just begun. Close the door, dear child, but open the window."

The two women left a short while later. Esmeralda promised to come back soon, while Sorcha said she'd see me the next day.

For the rest of that afternoon and evening, Montano's mother's words echoed in my head. Why would she say something had only just begun?

It was after seven when I picked up my laptop, sat on the bed, and wrote. Twelve hours later, I was still at it. I wasn't working on a new book. Instead, I was determined to finish the one Montano and I had started together.

33

Onyx

What I thought might be as simple as fixing Blanca's broken music box, or purchasing a new one, turned into one of the most difficult projects I'd ever undertaken.

Who knew carousel horses were carved by hand? Or that they started out as miniature replicas of what the full-size horse would be?

According to Al, the market for new carousels was nonexistent and had been since he was a young man. In order to generate an income, he'd started making music boxes from the prototypes.

Another thing I learned was there were cheaper versions to be had. Al had sold the rights to the designs shortly before he retired. However, those music boxes were not hand-carved like Blanca's was.

My hands bore the evidence of the scrapes and cuts resulting from learning how to work with Al's carving tools.

He and I usually worked first thing in the morning, and by ten or so, Al would be ready to call it a day, reminding me often that he was, after all, retired.

Since that left me with nothing to do for the majority of my time, I'd started work on Blanca's camp. It had been at Ranger's suggestion, buoyed by his brother, Jimmy, that I undertook the project of winterizing it for her.

Maisie had reopened Sherman's dance hall for a special event, and since it was so well-attended, they now had live music every Friday and Saturday night as well as Sunday afternoons. She pleaded with Jimmy and me to go with her and Ranger, but we turned her down.

My friendship with Jimmy had continued to grow to the point where I hung out with him more than his brother. It helped that we were both single, though I doubt he wanted to be any more than I did.

"What are we working on today?" he asked this morning like most when he'd see me come back from Al's place. Sometimes we opted for ice fishing, which we referred to as working for our dinner.

"You know next month is Blanca's birthday, right?" he said when I joined him out on the porch with a cup of coffee. Al abstained, saying he'd quit because of his high blood pressure. Maybe he was hinting I should do the same, but I loved the stuff.

Jimmy rarely brought Blanca or her late sister up in our conversations. Maybe his brother had warned him not to. Obviously, today was different.

"Yep, I sure do," I said, wishing I could forget how the only birthday I'd celebrated with Sofia was a huge letdown for her when all I'd planned was a nice dinner out.

"There was only one thing Blanca ever told me she wanted, not that I or anyone else could give it to her."

I let out a heavy sigh. "What was that?"

"A low-country swing. I guess they had one at their home in South Carolina that her father had built for her mother. The closest I ever got was hanging a hammock up for her that I think she slept in once."

I surveyed the porch, wondering where a swing would've fit if she'd ever gotten her wish.

"I hung the hammock over there," said Jimmy, pointing to the left side of the small space. He stood and looked up at the roof that had been extended from the main part of the camp when Blanca's father screened this part in. "In order for it to hold something as heavy as the swing, the roof would have to be shored up."

I shook my head. "Shoring it up wouldn't be enough, son. It would have to be reinforced with heavier supports and bigger beams."

"Right." He walked in the opposite direction, out the screen door, and around the front of the camp where the warm weather had melted the snow and made the ground muddy. "Looks like it wouldn't be that hard to do."

"When are you time traveling back to your teenage years to build her one?"

He came back inside, sat in the chair next to me, and rested his elbows on his knees. "You aren't the first person who wanted to preserve this place for Blanca."

"Look, I get that you were her knight in shining armor, but save it, son. I'm not interested in hearing about it."

He shook his head. "It wasn't me. It was Sofia."

Fuck if I wasn't finished with this conversation. Except Jimmy had said just enough to pique my curiosity. "What are you going on about?"

"Things got pretty rough for their family when Blanca's mom got sick. It was the summer before that when I hung the hammock for her. When we later heard that her mom had cancer, I got why she never asked her dad to build the swing.

"Anyway, it was her mother who'd inherited the camp from her family, and while they owned it free and clear, they almost lost it due to nonpayment of back taxes. I know my parents and some of the other lake residents tried to help, but Blanca's father wouldn't hear of it."

"You gonna tell me the rest of the story?" I asked after Jimmy didn't say anything more for several minutes.

"I never knew how much they owed, only that my parents heard Sofia worked three jobs over that summer to try to get the taxes caught up enough that the county wouldn't foreclose on them."

"She saved it for herself, not Blanca," I muttered.

"You'd think so, but you'd be wrong."

"How do you know?"

Jimmy sat up and sighed as heavily as I had a few minutes ago. "Something happened between Sofia and me. I'd rather not get into the particulars of it, but it ended in a big argument between us."

"Ranger told me she made a play for you."

Jimmy laughed. "That's one way to put it. Anyway, about a year later, I ran into her coming out of the county building not far from here, in Johnstown, where I was living at the time. I went in the opposite direction, hoping she hadn't seen me, but she called out to me."

When I got up and went inside, Jimmy followed.

"The conversation that day started off with her bad-mouthing Blanca, as you'd might expect, but when I went off on her about how she'd never be half the person her sister was—in my eyes or anyone else's—she broke down. I was mortified, to be honest with you. There we were, standing in front of the county building, and she was crying like I'd just broken up with her or something. I finally convinced her to go someplace more private where we could talk. That's when the rest of the truth came out."

I pulled a beer out of the fridge and held it out to him. When he took it, I knew this conversation was as hard on him as it was on me.

He twisted the cap off and took a swig. "She said she'd never liked coming to the lake, not like Blanca had. That's also when I found out Blanca wanted to be a writer. Sofia tried to play it off like her sister would be the happiest spending the rest of her life living with their parents, writing her 'stupid' books, while she had plans to make enough money to travel the world. She told me she'd enlisted in the Air Force and would one day be a pilot."

"That wasn't what Blanca wanted at all. She couldn't wait to get away from her family, especially after her mom died. She was the one who traveled the world." I suppose Sofia had too, but not in the same way. Sofia did it on the Air Force's dime—or United Russia's—while Blanca made her way in the world all on her own. But was almost losing the camp the reason Sofia was so obsessed with money?

"I asked her outright if the rumors were true, if she was the one who'd paid the back taxes. I could tell she didn't want to admit it, but she finally did. I asked her why her dad didn't just sell it. She told me he wanted to keep it for Blanca."

"Shit. That was harsh."

"No kidding. I asked how she felt about that, and her response was that she wanted her sister to have it too. She got up and walked away then, and I never saw either girl again."

"I don't think Blanca knows any of this."

"I'm sure you're right."

I thought back to when I'd hoped that when we found what Sofia left behind, it would turn out to be something just for Blanca. No evidence. No so-called insurance policy. Just something that would assure Blanca her twin loved her.

"She needs to know."

Jimmy tossed his empty beer bottle in the trash. "Yep. She sure does."

"You gonna tell her?"

"Nope. You are."

I still hadn't been given the all-clear to come out of lockdown—which for us meant we had to stick around Canada Lake or travel with an entourage. Since I hadn't been briefed on Blanca's location, I had no way to do what Jimmy suggested and tell her what her sister had done for her all those years ago.

The week after we first talked about the swing, Jimmy and I foraged around in the boathouse and found enough wood to build it. We also found a chain to hang it and some old boat cushions that could be used as a mattress.

"We could get these recovered," said Jimmy, trying to clean the dust off them.

"Where?"

"No clue, but I bet Mary would know."

Mary hadn't only known, she was the one to do the work. Two weeks later, we finished building the swing.

The same day Al and I completed the music box. Even I had to admit it turned out beautifully, despite my lack of woodcarving skills. It looked so much like the original, too. I wondered if Blanca would know the difference.

Whether she'd ever see it or use the swing she'd wanted for her birthday all those years ago, I'd probably never know.

"This looks great," said Jimmy, joining me for our daily cup of coffee. "What are we working on next?"

"I've run out of ideas. The camp is fully insulated now, with proper plumbing and electrical, plus a backup generator."

That wasn't all we'd done. The bathroom had been big, given all that was in it was a toilet and sink, so we added a walk-in shower and a bathtub. We'd talked about turning the loft upstairs into proper bedrooms, but that didn't feel right to me.

"Blanca has good memories of the sleepovers she had here," I'd said to Jimmy the day he mentioned the idea. His cheeks flushed, and he started to admit sneaking over to the girls' side, but I stopped him. "That wasn't one of her good memories, bro," I teased.

"We could start work on the boathouse," he suggested. "Get it ready for spring."

"Might as well. What else am I going to do?" I looked at the message on my phone. It was from Merrigan. She and Doc were on their way here and wanted me to assemble the team.

I couldn't decide whether or not that was good news. It might mean an agreement was made with United Russia that would end our sequestration. If that were the case, I'd be free to leave Canada Lake. The thought of doing so made my heart ache.

34

Blanca

"You made the right decision to return to your family's cabin. You will get the closure you need, I am sure of it," said Sorcha, walking me to the car, where her son and his wife were waiting.

"Please keep in touch," said Esmeralda, putting her hand on my shoulder. "I agree with Sorcha. This is for the best."

I nodded; part of me knew they were right. Would they have believed differently, though, if I'd told them the other reason I was going to the camp was to close the chapter on Montano too, or the significance of the day I was traveling there?

Perhaps if they had, they wouldn't be so certain I was doing the right thing.

"I appreciate this," I said to Merrigan when she and I boarded what looked like the same plane that brought me to the West Coast in December.

"We need to be in New York anyway, so it worked out nicely." She bent down and looked out the window. "Doc should be here shortly. He's meeting with the pilots."

I wanted to ask who they were, but they probably used different ones all the time. When I saw Wasp come through the cabin door, I smiled.

"Wow, it feels good to travel again," he said, cheek-kissing Merrigan first and then hugging me. Over his shoulder, I saw Swan board, go straight into the cockpit, but then come back out and approach Merrigan. By the way they greeted each other, it appeared they were longtime friends.

"Blanca, you know Swan, yes?"

"I do. Hello."

The woman stunned me by stepping forward and cheek-kissing me like I'd seen Wasp do with Merrigan.

"How are you holding up?" she asked, taking each of my hands in hers.

"Um, okay. Thanks." Her demeanor was so different from the last time I saw her; I didn't know what to make of it.

A few minutes later, she and Wasp returned to the cockpit, we settled in seats, and were on our way.

"Where will we be flying into?" I asked when we were more than an hour into the flight.

Merrigan's eyes opened wide. "My apologies. I never said, did I?"

"It's okay."

She stood from the seat next to her husband and sat beside me. "You have been a bit neglected, haven't you? We whisk you from one place to the next without even informing you of what's happening." Her cheeks turned bright red, and for a minute, I thought she might cry.

"It's fine. Really. I'm not upset."

"You should be. What I'm about to say isn't an excuse. Actually, it is, but I hope it will be more of an explanation."

I waited, unsure what else to say.

"These last several weeks have been very difficult for all of us. Until late last week, we believed everyone on our team, all the people who worked with and for us, along with their families, were in danger. Thanks to your sister, we were able to mitigate the threat we would've otherwise known nothing about."

I didn't know what to say. It was odd for me to hear something positive about my twin, especially lately.

"To answer your question, we'll be landing in Albany, at the same airport you departed from in December."

"Great. I can rent a car there."

"You can if you'd prefer, but it won't be necessary. We have meetings in the area."

"I think it would be best if I had my own." Although something else occurred to me. Had anyone returned my previous rental? "Um, I had a rental before when I was there."

"Another thing I should have made you aware of. We took care of it."

I supposed that much should've been obvious when I logged into my credit card account and had no balance due.

I rested my head against the seat, wondering if returning to the camp now was a good idea. Particularly today of all days. If we were flying to New York City, I'd do what I'd done before and spend a couple of nights there.

Although it didn't matter where I went or what I did. There'd be no escaping the fact that today was my birthday, which meant it was also Sofia's birthday.

How was it that I was turning thirty and my twin wasn't? I didn't know why this year felt different than last year, the first birthday I had without her, or even the years before. Was it just the milestone? It wasn't as though we'd celebrated a single birthday together since we turned eighteen. In fact, we hadn't even spoken.

Once we landed and were preparing to deboard, I hugged my bag close to me. Not only did it contain my laptop but something else very important. Something I hadn't decided whether I would share with anyone or keep for my eyes only for the rest of my life.

"Perhaps we'll see you tomorrow," Merrigan said when we walked to the rental garage together.

"This is me," I responded when I pressed the button on the key fob and one of the SUV's lights went on and off and the horn beeped.

When I pulled into the driveway that separated the Messick's camp from our family's, it didn't look as though anyone was at either place.

It wasn't until I got out that I heard music coming from the boathouse. And laughter. What was going on?

I opened the vehicle's back hatch, grabbed my bags, and set them on the ground. I was about to reach up to press the button to close it when a large, powerful arm beat me to it. I'd recognize that arm anywhere.

"This is a nice surprise," said Montano.

"Is it? Nice or a surprise?"

"Both. How are you, Blanca?"

Hmm. No angel. Okay. I guess we were back to business. "I'm fine, Montano. How are you?"

"I'm doing okay."

Before I could grab them myself, he slung my computer bag over his shoulder and picked up my suitcase.

"I can get that. It's fine. You must need to get back to work…or something."

He gave me a puzzled look. "What something do you think I'm doing?"

"I have no idea." He was toying with me, and I was in no mood. "Look, I'm tired, and I'd like to take a nap. If you wouldn't mind giving me my bags, I'll be out of your way." I looked beyond him then, to the camp I hadn't seen since December, and stopped in my tracks. "It's different," I mumbled.

"Not too different," he said, motioning for me to go ahead of him.

I didn't move. "I'm sorry. This is really awkward. I didn't expect to see you here. Quite honestly, the last several weeks of my life have been…surreal. I feel like I've been on a crazy ride, and all I want to do is get off."

"Like the Whip-it?" He smiled and I did too.

"Yeah, just like that."

I walked forward, but stopped by the porch steps when he did.

"There's something I need to tell you."

"Montano, can it wait? I'm sorry to be rude, but I really feel as though I need to lie down."

"Close your eyes."

"What? No." I put my hand on my hip. "What's going on?"

"Please. Just for a minute. I promise it will be worth it. At least I hope it will be."

God, I'd missed his little-boy charm, how he got so excited about the smallest things. Like ice cream. What was missing, though, was his usual swagger of confidence. Was he truly surprised I was here? Had he no idea I was coming? It was my camp, after all.

The way his eyes bored into mine, it seemed like he might kiss me. I definitely wasn't ready for that. "Okay, okay, I'll close my eyes."

"Promise to keep them closed?"

"Yes." I expected him to help me up the steps, but when he swept me up into his arms, I gasped and my eyes flew open.

"Come on. Close 'em."

"You could've warned me you were going to pick me up."

"Where's the fun in that?" He leaned forward enough that he could brush my lips with his, but he didn't. "Close your eyes, angel." The soft way he spoke was music to my ears that had longed to hear him call me that. "There we go."

He took two steps up and let go of me with one hand but managed to hold me steady with the other. I could hear the familiar squeak of the screen door.

"Meant to oil that," he mumbled.

I started to ask why he would since it was my camp, not his, but bit my lip instead.

"Oh, boy," he sighed. "I'm nervous." He set me on my feet and steadied me with his arm around my waist. "Okay, open."

For the second time in a few minutes, I gasped, looking at the swing hanging on the far end of the porch.

"It's beautiful." I rushed over and ran my hand over the bright-orange fabric of the cushion, the stained wood of the swing's arms, the sturdy black chain.

"Go ahead and sit on it. If it will hold me, it will hold you."

When my eyes met Montano's, his were beaming.

"How did you know?"

He took two steps closer. "I wish I could say I thought of it myself, but I didn't. Someone told me it might make a good gift. Happy birthday, angel."

I blinked my eyes several times, hoping to keep my tears from streaming down my cheeks, but it was pointless. "This is the nicest, sweetest, most wonderful gift. Thank you." I held onto the chain, sat on the cushion, and swung my legs up on the twin-size mattress. It gently swayed back and forth.

When Montano walked over to the camp's main door and reached inside, two heaters positioned above me came on.

"This way, you can be out here even if it's chilly."

From where I lay on the swing, I could see inside the bathroom window. Curtains were covering most of it, but there was something else in the room I didn't remember being there before.

"What is that?" I asked, pointing.

"Uh, it's a shower."

"You put a shower in my bathroom?"

Montano nodded. "A bathtub too."

I rested my head on the pillow, and he gave the swing a soft push.

"My father meant to do that, but then my mother got sick."

"I know. I found his plans."

"So does that mean there's regular plumbing?"

"Yep. Hot water and everything."

"Why?"

I saw the hurt in his eyes my question caused and patted the mattress. "Come lie with me."

"Are you sure?"

I tugged on the chains. "You built it. Think it can hold both of us?"

"I know it can. I meant, are you sure you want me to?"

"Yes, Montano, very much."

I sat up so he could put his arm around me and snuggled against him. "I'm sorry for asking why. I didn't mean to hurt your feelings."

"It's okay. I probably overstepped."

"Why did you?"

"There were a lot of reasons."

"I'm listening."

He smiled. "I was here, and like wherever you were, couldn't leave. Then Jimmy moved in, and we started—"

"Wait. Jimmy moved in?"

"Yeah. Goin' through a divorce. I wish I didn't have to tell you he'll be single soon, but I guess I do."

I laughed. "Let's leave Jimmy out of this for now."

"Anyway, he and Ranger suggested we winterize the camp at the very minimum. Then, we found your dad's plans and just kept going." He motioned with his head. "They're working on the boathouse now."

"Jimmy and Ranger?"

"That's right." He shifted a little. "Did you want to go say hello?"

I put my arm around his waist. "Not yet. First, tell me what else you did inside."

"That was about it. At least the stuff that's visible."

"Did you enclose the loft and make bedrooms?"

"No." He shook his head. "Maybe Jimmy was right. We should've. I just thought—"

I put my fingers on his lips. "You were right. I like the loft just the way it is."

He wrapped his hand around mine and kissed my fingertips. "I missed you so much," he whispered.

"I missed you too."

"You were pretty mad at me."

"I would've told you I forgave you, but someone shot you and you left."

He laughed.

I looked into his beautiful hazel eyes. "Thank God, you're okay, Montano."

"So, I've been here. Where have you been?"

"Butler Ranch."

He raised his eyebrows.

"I even spent time with your mother."

"Seriously?"

"Yep. She's the reason I'm here."

"Yeah? I had no idea she knew I was."

"I don't think she did." I told him about the conversations she and I had had about Sofia and how both his mom and Sorcha convinced me I needed to come back here. "Even if only one more time."

"I'm so glad you did."

"Me too. Although it made today harder."

"Your birthday?"

I nodded. "We were never here this early in the year. As you know, the camp wasn't winterized. Anyway, it wasn't like I had memories of being here with her other years on our birthdays."

"But it's still a place you spent time with her."

"Yes." I brushed a tear from my cheek. "Your mom gave me some more advice."

"Did she tell you I'm the most handsome, charming, thoughtful man you'll ever meet?"

"She didn't."

He put his hand on his heart. "Mama? You failed me."

"I knew already anyway."

He smiled. "What was the real advice she gave you?"

"She told me the music box itself wasn't what really mattered. She reminded me that I'd carry the memory of Sofia giving it to me with me for the rest of my life."

"Do you agree?"

"I do." I wished I could keep the sadness from my voice, but I'd probably never truly get over that precious gift being gone.

"Blanca, there are things I need to tell you."

"I know."

"Important things."

"I know that too."

He took a deep breath and let it out slowly. "Before I do, I want you to know I did this for you. The camp, the swing. It's all for you. I don't expect you to feel like you have to ask me to come visit or…you know, whatever. It's just for you."

"Hmm. Are you saying you wouldn't want to stay here with me?"

"That isn't what I meant. I just don't want you to think—"

"Because we have a big problem if you aren't planning to."

He turned so we were facing each other. "Yeah? What's that?"

"That isn't how the book ends."

"What do you mean?"

I scooted down the mattress so I could climb over him.

He flipped to his other side and watched me. "Where are you going?"

"Just over here. I'll be right back." I pulled the bound manuscript out of my bag and walked back over to the swing. Montano scooted over so I could lie next to him.

"What's this?" he asked when I handed it to him.

"Open the cover."

"*The Music Box*, written by Blanca Descanso and Montano Yáñez." He looked into my eyes. "Is this our story, angel?"

"It is."

"Can I read it?"

"You better. There's a scene near the end that I'm not sure works quite right." He picked up the book and flipped the pages. "No skipping to the end."

"But—"

"Nope, you have to start at the beginning."

35

Onyx

This was our story. It began the day Blanca came to my family's place in California, looking for answers about her twin sister. Answers I still hadn't given her, but I would.

She wrote about the tour boat in New York City, running through Central Park, visiting the Baseball Hall of Fame, and our time here at the camp and in Lake Placid.

I was familiar with that part of the book, and since she was reading over my shoulder, my angel suggested we go inside for it.

"Yeah?" I asked, hoping she was suggesting what I thought she was.

"Definitely."

I held open the door and waved her inside, remembering then that I had the other surprise in clear sight. "Blanca, wait."

When I heard her gasp, I knew it was too late. She'd seen it. I followed her in and wrapped my arm around her waist.

"Where did you get this?" she asked, carefully picking up the music box that sat on the dining room table. She ran her hands over every detail I'd hoped she'd notice, from the pink roses and ribbons that adorned the carousel horse to its blue eyes that Al insisted should be brown but I wouldn't relent. It was the one thing wrong with the music box Sofia gave her. On the actual horse, the eyes were blue.

She looked from it up to me. "Where, Montano?"

"I made it." Her eyes were questioning. "Well, Al made it, but I helped."

"I don't understand."

"I was surprised you didn't know this. Al's family owns the Jones Carousel Company. They built your favorite ride at Sherman's. More than that, though, Al's grandfather's name was Sherman Jones."

"I never knew."

I pulled her over to the sofa. "The year Sofia gave you the music box, she spent hours and hours working for Al, helping clean up his shop, whatever she could do to make enough money to be able to afford your gift."

"He told you that?"

I nodded, and when she started to cry, I pulled her into my arms. "There's more, angel." I held her as close as I could and told her the story Jimmy told me about how Sofia had paid the back taxes so they didn't lose the camp.

"It didn't end there, though. She kept paying them right up until she died."

Blanca looked stunned, so I gave her a minute to process what I'd told her. When Ranger said he'd done more research and discovered the taxes had been paid every year until last year, I'd been as surprised as Blanca appeared now.

"Thank you, Montano. You don't realize the gift you've given me." She stood, picked up the music box, and sat beside me. "Not just for this. Not for the swing or fixing up the camp. Thank you for giving my sister back to me."

And now came the time I had to take Sofia away once again. It would break Blanca's heart, but I had no choice. I couldn't keep what happened the day of the plane crash a secret any longer. I took the music box from her hands and set it on the table beside me.

"I'm not finished, angel. There's more you need to know."

She shook her head, moved away from me, stood, and walked over to the front door. She turned the lock, closed the front draperies, and flipped the switch for the outside heaters.

Instead of sitting beside me, Blanca held her hand out to me. I stood, and she led me into the bedroom.

"Don't forget our book," she said over her shoulder.

"Blanca, wait. We need—"

She spun around and put her fingers on my lips. "No more about my sister, Montano. Not tonight. Maybe not even tomorrow. We need to finish reading our book, and Sofia isn't in it."

"Tell me this much," I said, standing beside her near the bed. "Do we make love?"

"Oh, yes. In almost all the chapters."

36

Blanca

Montano and I spent most of the night making sure the scenes of our book worked as well in real life as they sounded on paper. My opinion, and his too, was they were far better. Just to be sure, though, we acted some of them out several times.

He had been right about us waiting until we were both ready for our lives to change forever the first time our bodies became one. I'd felt it last night and knew he had too.

I slipped out of bed and went into the kitchen. When we were in Lake Placid, Montano got up before me. He even brought me coffee in bed. Today, I'd do the same for him. I filled the teakettle, turned the fire on under it, and while the water came to a boil, put the coffee grounds in the bottom of the French press.

As I waited, I walked over to my music box, wound it up, and set it on the table, mesmerized by its beauty. I didn't think I could treasure it more, but knowing Montano helped make it, I did.

Like when Sofia gave me the same gift, it wasn't about going shopping, buying something that looked okay. This was about knowing the person the gift was for and doing everything to see to it they got it. In this case, I would cherish the love behind it as much as the gift itself.

And that was what it was truly about. Love. For all our disagreements, as different as we were, my sister loved me. Montano loved me too. He hadn't said the words, but he didn't need to in order for me to feel how much he cared about me.

The camp, the swing, the music box were all ways he showed me what words could never accurately convey.

Did he know I loved him too? I said it in the book, but I wanted to say it, to show him, like he'd done for me.

I raced over to the teakettle and took it off the heat right before it whistled. I poured it into the press, and while it steeped, I opened the curtains and looked out at the lake. When I arrived here yesterday, I didn't want to stay. Now, I never wanted to leave.

This was the view I wanted to see every morning when Montano and I woke naked in each other's arms and eventually started our day.

I looked out on the glassy water at the pair of loons cutting through it without leaving as much as a wake. There were few sounds more beautiful to me than that of a loon's cry.

"Good morning, angel," said Montano, putting his arm around my waist and his chin on my shoulder. "The loons have come to welcome you home. I haven't seen them in several days."

"I was just thinking there are few sounds I find more soothing." I looked over my shoulder and kissed him. "Hearing you call me angel is one of them."

"There are many, many sounds I can think of I love more, and I heard them all from you last night."

I reached up and put my hand on the side of his face. "There's one thing you didn't hear that I want you to."

He studied me.

"I love you, Montano."

He moved my hand from his face, but held onto it as he took a step back. As I waited for the words that didn't come, it felt as though a slow crack was working its way through my heart. "Blanca, we need to talk."

37

Onyx

"Okay," she whispered.

What I was about to do, I knew I had to, no matter how much I wished I didn't. Until I told her everything, I couldn't say the words I'd felt within days of meeting her. It's why I hadn't said it before now.

"I made coffee," she said, wriggling out of my grasp and walking into the kitchen. I watched, hoping she'd make eye contact, but she didn't.

"Let me get that," I said when she raised the press to pour the coffee but spilled it instead because her hands were shaking.

I poured two cups and set them on the coffee table. "Come and sit with me." I pulled her over to the sofa. When she sat too far for me to touch, I inched closer so the bare skin of our thighs kept us connected.

"Whatever you need to say, please just get it over with." Blanca folded her arms, but I pulled them from her body.

"I need to tell you what happened the day your sister died."

Her eyes opened wide and filled with tears. "Oh, God. No. I don't want to do this." Again, she tried to move away, but I wouldn't let her.

"We have to, angel."

She shook her head, but I had to get through this.

"We were both working a mission on behalf of K19 the day it happened. We'd been in Miami, waiting for word to deploy when the call came in on Thanksgiving morning, saying the two agents we were assigned to transport would be arriving within the hour."

Her eyes stayed focused on mine, even through her tears. I let out a deep breath and continued.

"The flight from Miami to Bogotá was routine until three hours in, when we hit bad weather over Aruba. The plane was getting tossed around pretty good, and when I tried to alter our course, I realized our radar system was down along with communication."

"You were flying the plane?"

"I was."

She nodded so I continued.

"Sofia reported there was a power grid failure in Venezuela causing us to lose our means to communicate with anyone on the ground, but something felt off to me. A few minutes later, she had manually entered our coordinates, and we were able to get ourselves out of the storm. At that point, I'd say we were less than an hour from Bogotá, and I needed a break. I turned to ask her to take over and came face-to-face with her gun."

"What?"

This was the hardest part because once I told her the last words I spoke to her sister, she'd never believe them when I said them to her. I had to do it, though. I couldn't live with myself if I didn't. If I lost her because she couldn't forgive me, I would be devastated, but neither of us could move forward with our relationship if I kept this secret any longer.

"Sofia's gun was pointed at me, and I knew that any second, she was going to shoot me."

"What did you do?"

"I told her I loved her, and she pulled the trigger."

"Wait. You didn't shoot her?"

"No. I did not."

"But she died."

"As I should have."

"What happened?"

"I was unconscious, but from what I've been told, one of the men we were transporting heard the gunshot and stormed the cockpit. Before Sofia could shoot him, he shot her. Given it was pilot-less, the plane took a dive. We all should've died that day. However, only Sofia did."

This time, when she tried to wriggle from my grasp, I let her.

"All along, you knew," she said, standing by the window and not looking at me. "You pretended like you didn't."

"You're right."

"But why?" Tears streamed down her cheeks. "Why didn't you just tell me?"

I wanted to pull her into my arms and beg her forgiveness, but this wasn't about me. I'd told Blanca the truth, the only secret that remained between us and would've threatened our future. Whatever conclusion she came to about us, I'd have to accept.

"Answer me."

"At first, it was because I couldn't. The details of what happened on that plane are classified. It's the reason no one you spoke with could tell you anything about the crash."

"You said at first."

"Things changed. While the mission remains top secret, I began to have feelings for you. And then, I wanted to protect you."

"I don't understand."

"When I promised to protect you, it wasn't just from danger, angel. It was from pain too."

"I see. You were protecting me."

"I told myself I was."

"Were you afraid I'd blame you?"

I shook my head. "I did nothing to warrant it."

"Do you know why she shot you?"

"What I've learned, only recently, is that your sister was a double agent. Her mission that day was to kill me along with the other two men on the plane with us. If everything had gone according to her plan, she would've landed the plane, probably in a remote location where the people she worked for would hide or destroy it."

"Do you believe my sister would've murdered three people in cold blood?"

"I do."

"Why?"

"I've subsequently learned she'd done it before."

"From what was on the SD card?"

"Yes."

"She left behind proof that she'd killed people?"

"What I believe is that she collected evidence in order to keep the people she worked for from killing her. It was an insurance policy of sorts."

"Why today, Montano? Why did you decide now was the perfect time? I mean, God, I just told you I loved you."

"I couldn't say it back to you until you knew the truth."

"You said that if my sister had lived, you wouldn't still be together. Is that because you would've found out she was a double agent?"

"No. It would've been because I'd already realized she and I weren't meant to be."

"Why did you tell her you loved her, then?"

"Because I believed those were my dying words. As close as she was to me, the shot should've killed me. Maybe somewhere deep in my soul, I wanted her to know the depth of her betrayal. Honestly, I don't know if I had time to think that much about it. I can't be sure why I said it."

"I'm going to ask you one question, and I want you to think about it before you respond. Tell me the absolute, God's honest truth, Montano. Do you love me?"

I walked over to where she stood, cupped her cheek with my palm, and looked into her eyes. "Blanca, I love you with every breath I take."

"I believe you."

"That simple?"

She pulled me back over to the sofa, and when I sat down, she crawled onto my lap. "You wouldn't ask if you heard the conversation I had with myself this morning."

"I wish I would've."

"I'll paraphrase. When I opened my eyes, everything I saw had your love in it. It isn't about fixing up my camp or building me a swing or even the music box. It's why you did those things. You did them because that's how much you love me."

"It is. It's exactly why."

Blanca rested her head on my shoulder. "Thank you for telling me about the plane crash."

"I had to."

"I know and I understand. More, I'm as glad as you are that we can put it behind us."

I hoped the day would come sooner rather than later when I stopped marveling at the ease of my relationship with Blanca compared to her sister or anyone else I'd been with. There was no comparison.

I'd said those words to her on the day I first called her my angel. Then and now, I felt them as much as I meant them.

"I think today we should finish our book."

Her eyes opened wide. "Finish it? It isn't yet?"

I shook my head. "Nope. There's one more chapter we need to write."

"Okay. Something beyond 'and they lived happily ever after'?"

I nodded. "You neglected to mention a very important detail."

"I'm so curious what that might be."

"The part where our hero asks our heroine to spend the rest of her life with him, to raise a family, and grow old together."

"What did she say when he asked?"

"She threw her arms around him and said, 'Yes, Montano, I will marry you.'"

"I *will* marry you, Montano, and I'll love you, with every breath I take."

We spent the rest of the day and night in each other's arms. We made love again and again, saying the words to each other as much as we showed them.

I checked my phone only once, to make sure I'd left it on, and was as relieved to find I had as much as I was that there were no messages.

There were things Blanca and I needed to talk about, including whether she wanted to return to Italy, but I didn't think it had to be decided right away. At least not until she brought it up.

"I want to live here," she blurted as we sat side by side at the table, eating a makeshift dinner.

"Yeah? I could get behind that idea."

"You could? I mean, could you live here too?"

"You said you'd marry me. That means you have to live with me too."

She rolled her eyes, something I found adorable. "What I meant is could you live here and still do your job?"

"I can," I said without hesitating. It was something Ranger and I had discussed more than once, and both of us believed it would be a good solution. "What about you? Can you write as well here as you did in Italy?"

Blanca popped an olive into her mouth. "I'll miss the food. Then again, I put on too much weight, staying with Sorcha and Laird." Even with her saying so, I didn't notice.

"Laird," I muttered, shaking my head.

"I know you call him Burns."

My eyes opened wide. "You do?"

She ate another olive and nodded. "Doc told me."

"You're practically a member of the family, then."

"They make everyone feel that way."

"Not everyone. Back to Italy. All you said was you'd miss the food."

"On the other hand, you can't find a good fish fry to save your life."

I smiled but leaned forward and looked into her eyes. "Blanca, you aren't answering my question."

"I can't say I'll never want to go back. I also can't say I'll ever want to leave Canada Lake."

I nodded, knowing exactly what she meant.

The next day, Doc sent a message that he and Merrigan would be stopping by midafternoon and wanted to meet with the rest of the "team" and me. I assumed that meant Ranger, Wasp, Cowboy, and Swan, although I had no idea who of the others was still in town besides Ranger and me.

If I was going to head up the shadow operations unit, knowing each member's twenty would be imperative. However, I was sure everyone would grant me grace for my last twenty-four hours of ignorant bliss.

"Ranger says you're supposed to go next door," Jimmy said when I heard his knock and let him in. "Hey, Blanca," he said, looking beyond me.

As I stepped aside and watched them embrace, the jealous feelings I'd anticipated didn't materialize, thankfully. I was a happy man and wanted to stay that way for as long as I could.

"Oh, Maisie is on her way over here too," he said, motioning to the other camp where I could see her and Ranger on the front porch. I turned away when I saw them kiss and walked over to Blanca to do the same to her.

"That's on, then?" I asked after Blanca kissed me back and then laughed and swatted my ass on her way into the bedroom.

"If you mean Maisie and Ranger, the answer is it's hot and heavy. She spends nearly every night over there."

I was happy for Ranger and would've said so if I didn't feel like I would be rubbing Jimmy's nose in it. He hadn't talked much about his ex-wife or their divorce, but it was obvious enough he was unhappy.

"Thanks for all you did to help Montano fix up the camp," Blanca said, returning from the bedroom wearing one of my sweatshirts over a pair of jeans. "And for telling him about the swing." She put her arm around my waist, and I put mine over her shoulders.

"You're welcome. I'm glad you finally got your birthday wish."

"Many birthdays' wishes," she said, beaming up at me.

"I'm really happy for you both."

At the same time Jimmy opened the door to let Maisie in, I saw two SUVs pull into the driveway. "That's my cue," I said, leaning down to kiss Blanca one more time.

38

Onyx

"How is Blanca?" Merrigan asked after we'd all said our hellos.

"I'd go so far as to say she's never been better," I said quietly enough that only she could hear me.

"I'm so glad. I take it that means you're feeling as she is?"

I leaned closer. "We're getting married."

Merrigan embraced me. "Onyx, I'm so happy for you both."

"You don't seem surprised."

She raised a brow. "I may be semi-retired and raising our family, however, I haven't lost my edge. You'd do well to remember that," she said with a wink.

I smiled. "Yes, ma'am."

Her expression changed. "We should get started. There's a lot we need to cover."

I took a seat when Doc asked everyone to, surprised when he came and sat in the chair beside me while Merrigan remained standing.

"This will be the one and only meeting I facilitate on behalf of our new unit, K19 Shadow Operations," she began. "After today, the team, along with its missions, will be in the hands of Onyx and Ranger." The small group applauded.

"By now you all should've received the final report on what we're referring to as the Flannery-Descanso mission. If there are any questions, I'll address them. However, I'd prefer not to spend more time than is necessary on it. Suffice to say United Russia will endure near-debilitating sanctions until the demands of the negotiators have been met. Including, but not limited to, the resignation and imprisonment of their leader. If he lives that long," she added under her breath.

I hadn't read the report, but if we weren't delving into its contents, I didn't understand why we were meeting. Before I could ask, Doc stood and handed an envelope to each person in the room other than Merrigan.

"What's this?" I asked.

"Your first official mission," he answered, opening his own envelope and pulling out its contents.

I did the same and read over the first few lines. When I looked up at Merrigan, she was studying me.

"What is this?" I asked, not understanding why we would be hired to conduct an investigation of a kidnapping and murder that would normally fall under the jurisdiction of local law enforcement if state lines hadn't been crossed and FBI jurisdiction if they had.

"We have been retained by the victims' families," Merrigan answered, evidently anticipating my confusion.

"Wait. Families?" I asked, turning the page to see there was more than one investigation involved. My eyes met Merrigan's again. "Three?"

"Yes," she said solemnly. "What we believe, is that there is a serial killer on the loose. One who is targeting the daughters of wealthy families in the area."

Area? I took a closer look. All three kidnappings and subsequent murders took place within the Adirondack State Park.

My eyes met Ranger's, and a chill came over me. He was on his way to the front door by the time I got to my feet.

"No!" I heard him shout, noticing the door of Blanca's camp was wide open.

Guns drawn, we entered the cabin while other members of the team went around the back. Once inside,

I raced over to Blanca who, along with Jimmy, was gagged, blindfolded, and bound to a chair.

"Where the hell is Maisie?" I heard Ranger shout at his brother, whom Wasp was untying.

"They took her," Blanca cried before Jimmy could answer.

Keep reading for a sneak peek at
Code Name: Ranger,
the first book in Heather Slade's
newest series,
K19 Shadow Operations Team One

1

Ranger

It was as though someone was tracking my thoughts. The moment the person briefing us on our next assignment said a serial killer was targeting daughters of wealthy families in the area, I thought of Maisie. She fit the victim profile better than anyone.

My eyes met those of my friend and boss, Onyx, who had to have been thinking the same thing I was, given he was on his feet, following me.

It defied logic, but my gut was telling me to get next door, where I'd left Maisie less than thirty minutes ago, and see with my own eyes that she was safe.

She had to be. My brother was with her. And Onyx's girlfriend. Or was she his fiancée? Either way, Maisie, Jimmy, and Blanca were fine. Once I confirmed it, I'd come back and we could resume our meeting.

"No!" I shouted when I saw the door to the camp wide open. Why was the fucking door open? It was the middle of winter.

I drew my gun as I raced through the doorway where my worst fears were confirmed. Both Jimmy and Blanca were gagged, blindfolded, and tied to chairs.

"Where the hell is Maisie?" I shouted at Jimmy, who one of the other guys in our unit was untying while Onyx did the same with Blanca.

"They took her," Blanca cried as soon as the gag was out of her mouth.

"Who?"

"Two men. Dressed all in black. Ski masks," Jimmy said between gasps of air.

"He's been hit," said Wasp, who'd untied him, pointing to the blood seeping into the fabric of my brother's shirt. I took a step to the side when Doc Butler, my boss' boss and a physician's assistant, rushed in to help Jimmy.

"Is there anything else you remember?" I could hear Onyx's words, but they were muffled by the roar of blood surging through my body. Every inch of my skin felt as though it was being pricked by a thousand pins as my brain triggered a fight-or-flight response.

I'd felt it before, more times than I could remember, but this was different. This wasn't fear for me. Someone took Maisie, and it was up to me to find her. Save her. Before it was too late.

About the Author

USA Today and Amazon Top 15 Bestselling Author Heather Slade writes shamelessly sexy, edge-of-your seat romantic suspense.

She gave herself the gift of writing a book for her own birthday one year. Forty-plus books later (and counting), she's having the time of her life.

The women Slade writes are self-confident, strong, with wills of their own, and hearts as big as the Colorado sky. The men are sublimely sexy, seductive alphas who rise to the challenge of capturing the sweet soul of a woman whose heart they'll hold in the palm of their hand forever. Add in a couple of neck-snapping twists and turns, a page-turning mystery, and a swoon-worthy HEA, and you'll be holding one of her books in your hands.

She loves to hear from my readers. You can contact her at heather@heatherslade.com

To keep up with her latest news and releases, please visit her website at www.heatherslade.com to sign up for her newsletter.

MORE FROM AUTHOR HEATHER SLADE

BUTLER RANCH
Kade's Worth
Brodie's Promise
Maddox's Truce
Naughton's Secret
Mercer's Vow
Kade's Return
Butler Ranch Christmas

WICKED WINEMAKERS
FIRST LABEL
Brix's Bid
Ridge's Release
Press' Passion
Zin's Sins
Tryst's Temptation

WICKED WINEMAKERS
SECOND LABEL
Beau's Beloved
Coming Soon:
Cru's Crush
Bones' Bliss
Snapper's Seduction
Kick's Kiss

ROARING FORK RANCH
Coming Soon:
Roaring Fork Wrangler
Roaring Fork Roughstock
Roaring Fork Rockstar
Roaring Fork Rooker
Roaring Fork Bridger

THE ROYAL AGENTS
OF MI6
Make Me Shiver
Drive Me Wilder
Feel My Pinch
Chase My Shadow
Find My Angel

K19 SECURITY
SOLUTIONS TEAM ONE
Razor's Edge
Gunner's Redemption
Mistletoe's Magic
Mantis' Desire
Dutch's Salvation

K19 SECURITY
SOLUTIONS TEAM TWO
Striker's Choice
Monk's Fire
Halo's Oath
Tackle's Honor
Onyx's Awakening

K19 SHADOW OPERATIONS
TEAM ONE
Code Name: Ranger
Code Name: Diesel
Code Name: Wasp
Code Name: Cowboy
Code Name: Mayhem

K19 ALLIED INTELLIGENCE
TEAM ONE
Code Name: Ares
Code Name: Cayman
Code Name: Poseidon
Code Name: Zeppelin
Code Name: Magnet

K19 ALLIED INTELLIGENCE
TEAM TWO
Coming Soon:
Code Name: Puck
Code Name: Michelangelo
Code Name: Typhon
Code Name: Hornet
Code Name: Reaper

PROTECTORS
UNDERCOVER
Undercover Agent
Undercover Emissary
Coming Soon:
Undercover Savior
Undercover Infidel
Undercover Assassin

THE INVINCIBLES
TEAM ONE
Decked
Edged
Grinded
Riled
Smoked

THE INVINCIBLES
TEAM TWO
Bucked
Irished
Sainted
Hammered
Ripped

THE UNSTOPPABLES
TEAM ONE
Furied
Married

COWBOYS OF
CRESTED BUTTE
A Cowboy Falls
A Cowboy's Dance
A Cowboy's Kiss
A Cowboy Stays
A Cowboy Wins